the road from prosperity

the road from prosperity

Stories

from

prosperity

Nancy Welch

Southern Methodist University Press

Dallas

This collection of stories is a work of fiction.
Names, characters, places, and incidents are either the product
of the author's imagination or are used fictitiously.

Requests for permission to reproduce material
from this work should be sent to:
Rights and Permissions
Southern Methodist University Press
PO Box 750415
Dallas, Texas 75275-0415

Cover photo: "Nothing to Do" by Bill Owens
Jacket and text design by Kellye Sanford

Library of Congress Cataloging-in-Publication Data

Welch, Nancy, 1963-
   The road from prosperity : stories / by Nancy Welch.— 1st ed.
   p. cm.
   Contents: Thanatology — The road from prosperity — Mental —
Running to Ethiopia — The cheating kind — Tender foot — Dog —
Lifeguarding — Texas sounds like an easy place to leave —
Sweet Maddy — Welcome to the neighborhood —
   The Good Humor man.
   ISBN 0-87074-499-2 (acid-free paper)
1. Ohio—Social life and customs—Fiction. 2. Working class families—Fiction.
3. Middle class families—Fiction. 4. Unemployed—Fiction. I. Title.

PS3623.E4625R63 2005
813'.6—dc22

                                                          2005041200

Printed in the United States of America on acid-free paper
         10   9   8   7   6   5   4   3   2   1

For Didier

Un peu. Beaucoup. A la folie.

Acknowledgments

Several of these stories, some in slightly different form, have appeared previously: "Thanatology" in *Green Mountains Review*, "The Road from Prosperity" in *Threepenny Review*, "Mental" in *Prairie Schooner*, "Running to Ethiopia" in *Mid-American Review*, "The Cheating Kind" and "Tender Foot" in *Other Voices*, "Lifeguarding" (published as "Deep Creek") in *Greensboro Review*, and "Sweet Maddy" in *13th Moon*.

Contents

Thanatology

I learned about death in a class called Thanatology, proposed by Mrs. Bauman, who also taught English and was married to the town's undertaker. The students of Prosperity High, Mrs. Bauman said, needed to learn a proper respect for death. Prosperity's pastors agreed, so long as her teaching never took a theological turn, interfering with their fierce competition to convince us that the Methodists and not the Pentecostals, or the Pentecostals and not the Lutherans, offered the true path to everlasting life. That seemed fine by her. Death and the English language—these were a science, or practical mechanics. In English class we read *Julius Caesar* and *A Tale of Two Cities* for the purpose of parsing each sentence.

"A sentence," Mrs. Bauman said, "is like a train. The subject is the engine. It pulls everything along. The period is the caboose."

At the word period the boys snickered, and those in the back made her words into their own lesson: "My cock is the engine, your cunt my caboose." They looked at me. "Whaddya say, Noreen? All aboard?"

That fall someone had etched into the orange paint on my locker *Noreen is a Nutsucker* because I was the only girl at school whose name began with "n."

"Choo-choo," the back-row boys chanted. "Now boarding Noreen Zacharias at track thirteen."

I was also the only girl whose last name put me in the back row. Mrs. Bauman seated all her classes in alphabetical order, and I approved of her consistency. Consistency wasn't something I'd seen much evidence of in adult behavior, so I considered it a virtue, one of the hardest to achieve. I ignored the boys and sat very still, my eyes stuck on a page of *To Kill a Mockingbird*. Scout tucked herself into Atticus's lap. Atticus told her something important and wise. I tried to imagine my own father, imagine he was a lawyer and a good man. It was a fantasy, and I understood that fantasies generally do not come true. That's why I liked Mrs. Bauman's English class, where we never talked about ideas and feelings. Ideas could take off like rockets; feelings sink you sure as stones. In Mrs. Bauman's English class we took apart sentences as if sentences were Tinkertoys.

"The verb form here is especially tricky," Mrs. Bauman said. "Who can identify it?"

Melodie Carver, sitting in the front row, raised her hand. At the same time she passed back a note. To Mrs. Bauman she said, "That would be the subjunctive." The back-row boys shut up. They smoothed out their note, sniffed it for a trace of Melodie's perfume. The note said: *Leave Noreen be.* Melodie passed back a second note. *Apologize.* One by one they did: *Sorry, sorry, didn't mean nothing by it, sorry.* I considered that if Melodie were to pass back a third note— *Shave your heads, wear sack cloth, spend the rest of your sorry days repenting in my name,* or *Blow dry your hair in a filled bath tub*—they'd have obeyed that too. Melodie had a halo of angel-blonde curls, a face that might come to you in a prayer. No one would write *Melodie is a motherfucker* on her locker just for the alliterative thrill.

Before the bell rang, Melodie passed back a final note. This one came to me, and it said, *Now do me a favor and tell your slut of a mother to keep her hands to herself.* The back-row boys watched with longing as I read my note. Donny Zimmerman, sitting beside me, sighed.

"Ever wish you was her?" he asked. "I bet you do. I bet all the girls do."

I shook my head. I never wished I was someone else. I knew from my mother where wishes could lead. My mother's name was Tish, and that's what she asked everyone to call her—no Missus or Ma'am or Mom for her.

"Be nice to Melodie," Tish would tell me. "She could be your sister one day."

"Stepsister," I'd reply, adding, "I think that's highly unlikely."

But nothing I said could faze her. She swept through the

house like it was the *Lawrence Welk Show*. She sat at her dresser each morning and curling-ironed her hair into a Farrah Fawcett flip. She put on dresses never meant to go to work—ones with deep Vs down the back and skirts that clung to her legs like needy children. Some months had passed since she'd remembered to ask, "How are you? How is school? How are you liking your teenage years?"

It's not that Tish paid no mind to me. She was just momentarily and giddily happy, unable to imagine that the whole wide world, even small children in the flood waters of Bangladesh, weren't happy too. Tish was having an affair with Larry Carver, Melodie's father, though she didn't like it when I put it that way. She said it made their love sound temporary and sordid. I told her she ought to consider that *temporary* at least was true. Larry owned the Buick-Olds dealership where Tish worked. She filed his contracts. Larry signed her paychecks. This affair was risky.

"It might not work out, you know," I told her. "It might be like the other times." I told Tish this because she seemed to have been born without the no-nonsense voice I often heard inside my own head, the one that said, *Snap out of it* and *In your dreams*.

"This isn't like the other times," Tish said, predictably.

My mother was an optimist. She believed we are not alone in the universe, that Prince Charles and Lady Di really were in love, that she herself had lived countless and fascinating lives. I tried reading to her from my Thanatology textbook. The book was called *Death: Facing the Facts.* It explained the five stages of decomposition, the use of the trocar to pierce and drain the heart. "Death," its opening sentence intoned, "is life's only certainty." Tish only waved a hand, gave a merry laugh.

She said, "Shouldn't you be reading *Romeo and Juliet?* Now there's a tale to pierce the heart. Or how about this poem—I forget who wrote it—I had to memorize when I was your age: *When thoughts of the last bitter hour,* something something, *Go forth under the open sky.*"

When I shook my head no, I'd never heard of such a poem, Tish said, "Be nice to Melodie. One day. You never know."

Mrs. Bauman wore thick theatrical makeup that appeared to be the same as her husband used on the dead. Rumor was that the blood had been drained from her body, her veins filled with formaldehyde. I felt sorry for her, though, on account of who she'd married. Mr. Bauman, who sometimes visited Thanatology as a guest lecturer, always said to the class in a weeping-willow voice, "The mortician's profession is a grave one." No one laughed, and even the back-row boys turned phantom pale. They said he did things with the bodies in the basement of the mortuary, the largest and finest of the Victorians on Main.

I believed this as much as I believed Mrs. Bauman bled formaldehyde, but there was no disputing that Mr. Bauman glowed at the sight of a good corpse the way some men glow before TVs tuned into Saturday-afternoon football or over the pages of *Playboy* magazine. Tish and I bumped into him one Saturday in the Sparkle Market. It was a cheery bright October morn two days after Donny Zimmerman—who had thought all girls must want to be Melodie Carver and perhaps wished he was himself—died on the railroad tracks behind the county fairgrounds. Mr. Bauman set a six-pack of Orange Crush and two boxes of Little Debbies on the conveyor belt.

"Watching the game today?" Tish asked.

Mr. Bauman shook his head. "Work day for me. This one's a project."

Thursday night Donny Zimmerman had stretched out on the railroad tracks to drink a fifth of sloe gin and maybe dream dreams of Melodie. He'd passed out sometime before the 10:50 came through. It was the kind of accident that happens when you mix alcohol with stupidity and a real blow to Mrs. Bauman, who'd sworn her course in Thanatology would make our yearbook the first in a decade not to dedicate itself to the dead. Donny's head had burst like a rotted cantaloupe, or so claimed the back-row boys.

"It's awful," Tish said. "About the Zimmerman boy."

"A train," Mr. Bauman agreed, "is no way to die. Terrible what it does to a body, let me tell you."

Mr. Bauman was tall, stooped, and of an age no one could determine. He might have been forty. He could have been sixty-two. His skin was the color of old celery, and his words usually trailed to the slow rhythm of a funeral dirge. Suddenly, though, in the checkout of the Sparkle Market, Mr. Bauman became animated. His words tumbled out one on top of the other, and if someone had asked, I would have said, yes, just then, Mr. Bauman's cheeks had bloom.

"I can usually work just fine with what I get," he said. "And folks like to see in a poor soul's face some indication they died seeing the Savior or their boyhood dog. I can understand. I can oblige. But the Zimmerman boy. I won't describe. You can imagine. Hard to make it look like he saw anything at the last but several hundred tons of speeding steel getting ready to give him the hug of his life."

Beside me Tish looked green.

"I heard he was stone-cold out," I put in. "I heard he couldn't have felt or seen anything."

"Oh," Tish said. "I didn't consider that." She sounded disappointed, as if she'd imagined Donny wide-eyed awake, the train's high whistle drowning out his moans of "Melodie, Melodie, my halo-headed Melodie."

Mr. Bauman was packing the Orange Crush and Little Debbies into a paper sack. He paused, gave the top of my head a pat, and I would have shivered, thinking where that hand had been, except just then he had sounded like any man deeply in love with his work, like Larry Carver going on about Buicks as if Buicks were bound to save us all.

Later Tish told the story to Larry. We sat at the kitchen table, Tish and Larry drinking cups of coffee and me studying for Monday's quiz in Thanatology. Tish wore a dress ready to celebrate New Year's Eve. Larry's hands jittered about his coffee cup. Outside a car backfired. He popped up in his chair, and a splash of coffee landed on his shirt.

"Why are you so jumpy?" I once asked him.

"It's your mother," he'd replied. "She could make any man shake."

"Damn kids," Larry said now as the backfiring car gunned down the street. "Least Noreen here has her priorities straight."

"Mrs. Bauman said Noreen can really parse," Tish said, proudly. "She said Noreen has a definite future in the funeral industry." She paused. "Not that Noreen will pursue that line of work."

"Bill Bauman is not a well man," Larry said. "It's all those chemicals, I suppose."

"He spoke very kindly to us today," Tish said. People didn't often speak kindly to Tish. Most women in Prosperity wouldn't give her the time of day. That's how they put it and in voices loud enough for Tish to hear, as if the time of day was something particularly precious that they alone had. I couldn't really despise Larry. Since Tish had started working for him six months before, after U.S. Steel over in Elyria shut down and put half of Prosperity out of work, he'd been kind to us too. He treated me as a sturdy adult. "We both want what's best for your mother," he would begin, then ask my opinion on her hours or which Buick she should drive, its sides emblazoned with *Carve Out Your Deal at Carver's Buick and Olds.* At the time, Tish had been going with Eugene Bender, who owned the local Culligan franchise and had on his right hand a twitchy sixth finger. Together Larry and I fretted as if Tish were the teenager and not me.

"Eugene's employed," I had pointed out. I could think of instances where this had not been the case.

"There's that," Larry had agreed.

"He's not a holy roller," I added. Tish could not resist a man who spoke in tongues.

"And the extra finger," I told Larry, "isn't really Eugene's fault."

We would sit in his office, me in his big leather chair, my feet up on the desk Tish Pledged every day. Framed photographs scattered across the desktop: Larry's family in hooded parkas looking like they were born wearing skis, Larry's family in swimsuits waving from a boat.

Sometimes Tish sailed into the office, stopped, looked from Larry to me and back again.

"What are you two looking so serious about?"

"Grammar," Larry would reply.

"Grammar," I would echo.

"I've just been explaining to Noreen here that without grammar, not a one of us could make sense."

"No sense at all," I agreed.

Lingering over Larry's desk, Tish fingered the edges of the photograph frames.

"We should take a vacation," she murmured. "See Niagara

Falls, the Baseball Hall of Fame, or why think so small? Why not the Grand Canyon?"

"I'd like to go to Cedar Point," I told her. Admission to all the rides and a view of Lake Erie was only twelve dollars a day. "Let's go there," I told her, "like last year."

"I can get you in for free," Larry offered. "We give free admission to everyone who buys a new car here." He smiled fondly at Tish. He looked at her in a way I'd never seen him look at his own wife, who was an older, slightly plumper version of Melodie. "Not that I would make you buy a new car, of course," he added.

With Larry, Tish claimed, the phrase *heart of gold* was more than a metaphor, and when Eugene Bender announced that he'd started attending Wednesday night Bible studies and had met there a young woman with a sixth toe, she didn't give a single boo-hoo. God, she'd told him, had reached a gentle hand into her life too. In Tish's mind it could have been so: the hand of God shutting down U.S. Steel and guiding her toward Carver Buick and Olds even though Larry hadn't advertised for an administrative assistant, hadn't dreamed he needed one until the day my mother stepped through the dealership door. That's how Tish worked on men. They never imagined that the fulfillment of their hopes, the answers to their prayers, might come to them so easy and so sweet. Until they spotted Tish and thought, "Yes. Maybe this. Maybe her." So it must have been with Larry that day he laid eyes on Tish and considered that an affair with such a woman didn't have to be in his dreams.

After lunch that Saturday, Larry excused himself from the kitchen table, saying he would check on the living-room light. The week before it had blown its bulb with a sudden pop and a worrisome wisp of smoke, and when I said I'd call an electrician, Tish had said no, we'd let Larry take a look. As she explained it, Larry, like any man, needed—in case God or his wife should inquire—some kind of excuse. Larry was a deacon at the United Methodist, and sometimes he eyed me like I was sitting in judgment on him. I wanted to tell him I wasn't, I really wasn't, I just had no reason to suppose he wouldn't take off fast as my own father had. My father had been a salesman for the Royal Typewriting Company. One day he'd left for a sales trip to Indiana, then sent Tish word he wasn't coming back. No one, he said, wanted Royal Typewriters anyhow. Not when they could have IBM Selectrics. His future, the note said, was in Terre Haute.

"Why don't you go chat with Larry," Tish said. She tucked lunch dishes into the sink, out of sight. "Keep him company."

I nodded. Larry and I visited every week, though not like before when both of us clearly had Tish's best interests in mind.

"How's Mrs. Carver?" I asked him.

He toppled on the ladder step. Then he steadied himself.

"Fine," he said.

"She used to direct my Girl Scout troop. She taught me how to put out a campfire."

Larry busied himself with the wires.

"That's a useful thing to know," I said. "How to put out a fire."

He seemed to be making a mess. A dozen rainbow-colored wires dangled from the hole in the ceiling. He frowned at the wires and didn't reply.

"I hear Melodie was voted harvest queen by the Future Farmers of America. That's a real honor, seeing how she's only a sophomore."

One of the wires hissed against Larry's fingers. He jumped, nearly fell a second time.

"You must be very proud of her," I persisted. I wanted to add that I was sorry to bring up something that might cause him to fall, break his neck. I really was. I wanted to add that I wished sometime we could sit down face-to-face and hash this thing out like the two adults we supposedly were.

"What are you two talking so seriously about?" Tish glided into the room. She stretched a gingham-checked dish towel before her like a dancing partner. Larry stopped sucking on his zapped fingers. We looked at Tish. She danced as if the dish towel were a graceful, handsome man. She danced in a way that could have held us there, bewitched, for the rest of the afternoon. Then she stopped, dropped the towel to her side.

"Well?" she said. "Fill me in."

"History of electricity," Larry replied.

"Yes," I said. "Larry's been explaining to me about Benjamin Franklin."

"And Thomas Edison, G.E., and American know-how," Larry continued. "Just think, sweetheart, without them, we'd all be in the dark."

He looked at me, and I looked back, not blinking until he did. He returned to fiddling with the wires, poo-pooing Tish when she asked if he wasn't in danger of frying himself. He told us about the new Buicks due in the showroom December 1. They'd have Japanese engineering and made-in-the-USA parts. They'd be the safest cars on earth, sealed up tighter than any tomb.

"It's all about physics," Larry said. "It's about mastering the laws of the universe before they master you."

He pointed at the hole in the ceiling.

"This one's a project," he said. "It'll take me another Saturday."

For the rest of that fall this went on, Larry appearing every Saturday for lunch and to repair something that had broken during the week. Our house was a clapboard two-story in a neighborhood where long poles propped up sagging eaves and cinder blocks replaced rotted front steps. As a child I'd taken my afternoon naps to the busy sounds of saws and hammers or the clang-clang-clang as my father went to work on our pipes. U.S. Steel and Fisher Body burst with business, and people wanted my father's typewriters just for the royal ring of the name. From the broken-down coal mines of Kentucky and Tennessee, whole families migrated, grannies in tow, drawn to northern Ohio by the smell of steady jobs. Prosperity, Ohio, which I learned in school had once been the Limburger cheese capital of the world, was making a comeback. So sang all those busy hammers and saws until, over the months and years, the hum of thirty men at work on their homes dropped to fifteen, ten, and then one all alone, making a racket instead of a song. Plywood went up over the plate-glass display windows of Wannamaker's Pharmacy and the Farm and Home. At Sparkle Market you could sign a petition against the opening of a Food-4-Less.

"Maybe I should just sell this place," Tish would sometimes say to Larry. "I could get an apartment in that complex out by the highway. You know, by the Bob Evans? The one with the pool?"

Larry vigorously disagreed. "Ownership," he would reply. "Equity. You can't beat that."

Larry was still paying on his house. And on the boat, a Lake Erie cottage, and a time-share at Myrtle Beach. "I pay," he once told me grimly over his desk at the dealership. "And pay and pay and pay."

He'd had his house custom-built in a development called Country Club Acres, the name just a wish since Prosperity

had never proved prosperous enough for golf. Saturdays
after lunch, I would take a long walk through Country Club
Acres, though I couldn't tell which custom-built house was
Larry's. They all looked the same with colonial columns and
lawns rolling undisturbed to the street as if children there
did not play kick-the-can. Coming back through what
remained of downtown, my feet shuffling slow so I would-
n't reach home before Larry had gone, I parsed signs: *Get
Your John Deere Snow Blowers Here; At Sparkle Market, You'll
Find a Sparkling Smile in Every Aisle; In Your Hour of Need
You Need the Bauman Funeral Home.* Each sign had *you* as
its subject—a *you* whose vast, vague hunger just might be
satisfied by a new snow blower or soothed by the capable
hands of Bill Bauman. After Thanksgiving, banners
appeared in the wide windows of the Buick-Olds showroom
declaring *Sale, Sale, Sale* and *Leave Our Keys Under the Tree.*

In Thanatology I was learning that when you die, your
body releases enzymes that eat you away from the inside
out. I learned that embalming isn't just an art, it's a necessity. Mrs. Bauman passed around eye caps, mouth-formers,
the terrible trocar. The back-row boys tossed the trocar
about like a javelin.

"Hey Noreen," they said, waggling their eyebrows. "What
we got for you is longer than this."

I stayed still and tried to imagine that my father wasn't in
Terre Haute but Angola, doing fifteen to twenty for armed
robbery and telling the other inmates the only decent thing

he'd done was make me. Then I recalled Tish telling me that my father had suffered from bleeding gums. In class Melodie no longer stuck up for me. She passed back notes that said, *I hope your mother gets vagina rot* and *Everyone knows you have lice.* Finally I passed words of my own down the rows to her. *Don't worry,* I wrote. *It won't last for long.*

At lunch the Saturday before, Larry had turned down pie for dessert. Tugging at the waist of his pants, he'd said, "My wife is threatening to put me on a diet." With increasing frequency, I knew, Larry would let slip the names of his wife and two children, the bare facts of his multiple mortgages, his numerous and weighty obligations. His hands no longer jittered when Tish was about. She could make any man shake, but only for so long. Any day I expected to come home from my Saturday afternoon walk, find her alone at the table, her sobs a dry cough because she'd been at it for hours. Tish never saw it coming, never learned from the last time.

"You can do better," I would tell her. "He doesn't know what he just passed by."

Before Larry there'd been Eugene and before Eugene there had been young Doctor Bird who had cleaned my teeth twice for free before his wife found out and I had to return to old Doctor Pitts who enjoyed quoting from the Book of Job and did not believe in Novocain. After Doctor Bird, Tish had declared, there could never be another. He'd taken with him her heart along with two of her wisdom teeth. I imagined making for Tish a weekly vocabulary list, the words she had never learned like *bemused, ironic, perspective.* Or I would take one of her oft-repeated sentences— "But Larry (or Eugene or young Doctor Bird who even in bed likely preferred to be called Doctor) is different." I would take such a sentence, parse it, show her that no matter who the man is, the grammar remains the same.

"You fall in love too easy," I told her. "You fall in love like other people brush their teeth."

"Maybe that's a virtue," Tish replied.

"A man who loved you would stay the night," I pointed out. "He'd stay longer than half an afternoon."

"Time is told not by the clock," Tish answered. She smiled. "Doesn't that sound like a poem? Like a sonnet someone famous wrote?"

I couldn't say. We studied no sonnets in Mrs. Bauman's English class. She'd recently introduced us to William Cullen Bryant's "Thanatopsis," the poem Tish had recalled in mangled bits from her childhood, but only to make the point that Mr. Bryant's verse suffered from slight acquaintance with actual facts about his chosen subject. I told Tish never mind poetry, we should take stock of what we had—front steps, strong teeth—write it down, call it enough. Wishes, I told Tish, are like the enzymes I learned about in Thanatology. They eat away at the soft lining of the stomach, the once-strong wall of the heart. At Saturday lunch I'd catch the wishes warming Larry's face like sunshine on bed-

sheets. For a minute he'd forget his wife, his house, sales at
the dealership that had sagged just the same as the houses
on our street. He'd rest his chin in his palm, watch Tish at
the sink, his face suddenly soft as clouds. But then a car
would backfire or from a nearby porch a woman would call
her child's name. At that Larry would snap up straight. He'd
blink, clear his throat, give his head a sharp shake. At such
moments he too heard the voice Tish had been born without: *Snap out of it. In your dreams.*

   There are times when I can imagine another ending, those
wishes settling deep within Larry's heart and refusing to
budge. "I almost married her," Larry said at Tish's funeral five
years later. Then again, so did Doctor Bird, Eugene Bender,
two of the three men who followed Larry, and even my own
father come all the way from Terre Haute to consider, "I
almost stayed. I almost came back." Who can say if one of
these might have been the saving story for Tish? A story
telling her that every bit as real as her belief in the true love
of Prince Charles and Lady Di was the growing lump on her
right breast. A story telling her to never mind the question of
life on Mars and spend some time tending to her own.
   "Noreen is my most consistent and responsible pupil,"
Mrs. Bauman once wrote on a progress report, though
whether for her class in English or the one in death, I could-
n't say for sure. In memory the two courses braid tightly into
one. In all things I was consistent, perhaps in all ways

responsible. I took my mother's affair with Larry Carver into my own two bone-dry hands.

"We both want what's best for Tish," I said to Larry the last Saturday he came. We were in the upstairs bathroom, Larry hunkered down beside the toilet I suspected Tish of clogging with a pair of pantyhose just to give him something to repair.

"And you got your business to think of. Your wife. The house, the cottage, the time-share. And Melodie. Think of her."

I handed him the plunger and he took it, sadly.

"I thought maybe we could go on just as we are," he said.

"Everything dies," I told him, and when I started to explain the stages of decomposition, relating each to his failing love for Tish, he held up a hand. He said lately the hymns he sang at church made him shake. I didn't point out that once upon a time Tish could do the same.

He said, "I really did want to make her happy."

"But you can't," I said.

"We're talking laws of the universe," I concluded. "You know what you got to do."

"You'll help me?" he asked.

"Of course."

I added, "She needs to keep her job."

"I wouldn't dream otherwise," Larry said. "Or I could line up work for her someplace else. Jack's Toyota. Toyotas seem to be selling these days."

He glowered. "Jack'll probably thank me for it."

"There's more," I told him.

"More?" he said.

I nodded. *More.*

When we came downstairs, Tish met us at the landing. She looked from Larry to me and back. "What have you two been talking about up there?" Her smile was bright, her voice strangely high.

"History of plumbing," Larry replied briskly.

"Yes," I said. "It all started in ancient Rome."

"Toilet's all fixed," Larry added. He didn't say it was a project. He didn't say it would take another Saturday.

That night I dreamed of Terre Haute. I dreamed Terre Haute looked exactly like Prosperity except with a Taco John's instead of Bob Evans and a wind that blew steady, making the whole town creak. I awoke with my heart crying out, "Don't you hear it? Doesn't anyone hear it?" The creak, I realized, came from down the hall, Tish's room. I found her, knees pressed into the floorboards, hands folded beneath her chin, her forehead butting the bedcovers as if she was a small and hungry calf. Once when Tish was seeing a tongue-speaking man, she'd taken us to the Divine Word and Faith Redeeming Holy Tabernacle in an empty down-town store that used to offer one-hour Martinizing. For three months she'd worn no makeup or colors brighter than gray or brown. She'd asked me to call her Mother, which I did not like, missing the flirty dresses, the flipped and feathered hair. Sometimes the tiny congregation would lay hands on a member fevered with prayer, and on that night, that's what I did. I lay hands on Tish's forehead not to join her in the spirit but to see if she was sick.

"I'm just being silly," Tish said, crawling back under the covers and shaking her head when I brought aspirin. She took the glass of water and drank it down as if her prayers had taken her to a desert.

"What were you praying for?" I whispered.

"For a change," Tish replied. "Why else would someone pray?"

"What kind of change?"

I thought of the deal I'd made that afternoon with Larry and that Tish had not yet heard of. I thought of her fluttering about the house in the weeks to come, restless as a hummingbird and maybe changing the color of her hair. I wondered who would be next, whose hands would jitter, then stop, as he too got used to her, started to wonder why he was sitting in our kitchen when he could be home watching football or mowing his lawn.

"Snow," Tish said. "I'm praying for snow."

I nodded. Snow made everything in Prosperity appear equal. Whether you lived on Main Street or in Country Club Acres, in the one of the tar-papered shacks out by the fairgrounds or on our street in between—snow made it all look restfully the same.

"Talk to me?" Tish asked. Her voice was small like a child's. "Tell me what you'd pray for."

Instead I told her that the next summer when I got my license, we'd rent a shiny new car—no, a convertible—and drive to Utah, Nevada, places we'd never been.

"Where'd we get the money for that?" Tish asked.

"Don't worry," I told her. "We'll have it."

"I only get a week's vacation," she pointed out.

"By next summer," I promised, "you'll have more. Or for now, let's just pretend."

I went on, Tish quiet, listening as I told her all we would see: amber waves of grain, purple mountains, smiling folks in overalls and pretty cotton dresses drinking cold pop from green bottles. I told her we would head south. We'd drive deep in the heart of Texas while singing "Deep in the Heart of Texas." We'd hit Oklahoma just as the sun came up, sing "Oh! What a Beautiful Morning," then arrive in Topeka in time for lunch at a picnic table with a checkered cloth. I shivered, remembering my dream about Terre Haute. Maybe the whole country looked like Terre Haute, and "America the Beautiful" was only a song people believed because they hadn't driven from sea to shining sea to find out for themselves. I thought about Mr. Bauman in the mortuary basement laboring to make each face look peacefully resigned at the last even though maybe how people really died was this: They glimpse in the end not pearly gates, gossamer angel wings, or a host of halo-headed Melodies but

Taco Johns and Buick-Olds showrooms. In heaven there would be acres upon God's-country-club acres of custom-built homes that all look the same so people spend eternity going from door to door, trying their key, ringing the bell. In the hereafter there'd be sales, sales, sales, men who'd say, "I thought I wanted you, but maybe I want a John Deere snow blower instead," and young Donny Zimmermans trying every way to mix a lethal dose of alcohol and stupidity even though this was heaven and so presumably they were already dead. One look at this could stop your pulse. The truth—the real stuff, not the twisted syntax that can't be parsed—can pierce, can drain, the heart. You look. You think, "So that's it" and "So that's all," heaven just more of the same ceaseless hungry hope.

"Go on." That's what Tish said. "It sounds wonderful."

That's when I realized I'd skipped New Mexico, so I circled us back, told her about cactus flowers that bloom when the sky is the color of India ink, the strange music of the desert at dusk. I knew nothing about this. I was making it all up, lying my head off, lying so well I almost believed it, could hear the music, smell the sweet perfume. I told Tish we would find happiness. I told her we would find love. I told her it was out there, that all we had to do was look.

"And pay," Tish said.

Her voice was so faint, I wasn't sure I'd heard her right.

"What was that?"

"You heard me. He won't be coming back. I could tell, the

way he ducked out the door, fixing on his shoes like he expected them to speak."

She propped herself up on an elbow, studied my face as if I should speak, as if she knew there was something I ought to say. All the pretty pictures in my mind withered away. No music, no flowers, no power of the imagination to alter basic facts. Just the tick of the nightstand clock, a voice in both our heads insisting *What's the sense of having dreams.*

Then she smiled. Or grimaced. In the dark it was hard to tell.

"But go on," she said. "Tell me where we can go next."

The Road from Prosperity

In Cincinnati the snow changed to rain. It was midnight, the sky foggy, but the highway swirled with lights: headlights, turn signals, a sudden flash of brakes. Portia's headlights didn't seem to be working. She couldn't see the lines that marked her lane. On both sides cars and semis swept past, sending up sprays of slush and stone. She thought about Walter. He was a boy at school she'd hardly known, dead now. She thought of him as an angel in billowy white with thick-lensed glasses slipping down his skinny nose. She imagined he hovered close by, his delicate hand reaching out to steady the wheel.

Except Walter had been Catholic. And if you were Catholic and a suicide, you couldn't be an angel.

If there had been an exit then, she would have taken it. She would have turned around and returned to Prosperity with its glassy air and icy stillness. She'd have welcomed the bump of her wheels over railroad tracks, the sight of snow-shrouded Victorians lining Main Street.

But suddenly Cincinnati lay behind her, and the Olsons' Oldsmobile carried her over the Ohio River and into the dark hills of Kentucky. The road ahead was wide, straight, and empty. Turning on the radio, Portia bobbed her head to Springsteen. He sang about wasted dreams and squealing cars. On the seat of his car, Portia's father, a salesman, kept a drum brush, and as he drove around the country, he swish-tapped to Sinatra or the Ink Spots. Her mother would re-mind him that instead of driving, he could take a plane; it would get him home more often. But he asked if she'd ever heard Willie Nelson sing "In the Air Again." Of course not. Planes had no feeling. Planes had no romance.

Portia could imagine him right now, somewhere out there in the night, swish-tapping and singing "My Way." And as she followed the road that led south from Prosperity, she sang "Born to Run." She imagined she was Wendy, some backstreet girl riding out to the Promised Land with a boy like Bruce at the wheel.

In a rest area bathroom somewhere near Louisville, a toi-let behind her flushed, and a voice like gravel muttered, "Damn john's a block of ice." In the mirror she watched a woman move up to the sink beside her. The woman had gray hair coiled into a bun, and she wore a brown buttoned cardigan that puckered around her middle. She smiled at Portia as she bent to wash her hands. Portia smiled back.

"Can't wait to get where it's warm," Portia said.

Then wished she could swallow those words because the woman answered, "Oh? Where you headed?"

Portia ducked her head and searched the bottom of her purse for the car keys. Maybe this woman had heard radio news broadcasts alerting people to be on the watch for a teenage girl in a stolen car. But no. What she'd done wasn't big enough, dramatic enough, to earn a news flash. Maybe not even a call to her father. She looked up at the woman and said, "Florida. For spring break. My grandmother lives there." It surprised her, how easily that lie slipped into words and seemed to be true.

The woman laughed. "Winter break, they should call it. What college you go to?"

"M.I.T.," Portia said, which was where her brother, Bill, had applied in case he didn't get into West Point.

"*Jesus,*" the woman whistled. "A future rocket scientist."

"Actually, my field is artificial intelligence." Artificial intelligence was her brother's major.

The woman arched her brows, looked impressed, and Portia felt an electric thrill. She was nobody. She could be anybody. A designer of robots. A builder of rockets.

"My name's Patricia," she said, holding out her hand. "But my friends call me Patty."

"Patty," the woman repeated, smiling at her.

Portia liked the sound of that name, so cheerful, so normal, and she was glad she'd picked it instead of Mercedes, which was her second choice. As they headed back to their cars, she told the woman she was the sophomore class president, a literacy volunteer, and yes, that did keep her busy but still she found time to study and earn straight As. The woman sighed and said she should talk to her grandson. He was smoking pot and failing the tenth grade.

Portia shook her head sadly. "That's too bad." For a moment it really seemed so.

She thought about her father as she headed south. On the road he too could be anybody, shedding his name, his family, his whole history just as easy as a snake sheds its skin. Maybe right now he sat in a Holiday Inn lounge in Provo, Utah, telling the bartender he was the ambassador to Thailand and not a seller of machine lubricants. Or he fingered cards in a riverboat casino, a rakish gambler rather than a family man from Prosperity, Ohio. On the road, she imagined, he greeted each day with a wink and a grin. Under his wheels all the mundane worries scattered like tiny pebbles: canceled accounts, missed quotas, a wife who'd taken a job—*Because someone around here has to think about the future*—without even asking.

Though Portia didn't know for sure just where he was. The morning she left, her mother woke her, saying, "I'm leaving for work now. You better get up. The roads are bad." Looking outside, Portia saw elm branches stretching dark against slate sky, the rooftops dusted in white. On the radio Springsteen sang "Thunder Road," and she looked down and saw the Olsons' Oldsmobile sitting in the driveway beneath their closed shades. She paused, thinking about issues like Theft and Morality. Her Office Procedures teacher had once lectured the girls on Office Ethics, saying, "Remember, taking even a pair of scissors is a serious crime." But there was her father too, all he had told her about the romance of a fast car on an open road. She didn't know if the Olsons' car would be fast, but she figured it would have cruise control.

Before tiptoeing out to see if the key was, according to small town habit, in the ignition, Portia stopped by the dresser in her parents' room. She looked for the notepad that would show her father's number for the week—his neat block print, the solid words Ramada Inn Providence or Sheraton Tampa. But the dresser was nearly bare. Just an empty pack of Salems and, closed in its velvet-lined case, her mother's diamond watch. The watch had been a long-ago gift from her father, never worn—it was, her mother said, much too extravagant, much too nice—but always, like keys in cars, sitting there.

At a gas station near the Tennessee border, she heard the thin whine of a distant radio, a voice singing about heartache, betrayal, and loss. It was just past three A.M., and in a flash of inspiration, Portia told the boy at the pump that Loretta was a good friend of hers. She said she was Desiree Dalton and she was a country singer.

"Yeah, sure," the boy said, turning on his boot heel and

unscrewing the gas cap. "You can't even be eighteen years old," he said.

"Tanya Tucker was just thirteen when she had her first hit," she pointed out. Her father had taken her to see Tanya, a child in black leather pants, at the Ohio State Fair. "That could be you," he'd told her. "Can you sing?"

"Hey," she called to the boy. "Listen to this." And with a deep breath, she began: *Oh, give me land, lots of land, under starry skies above.* The boy turned, stared, and she pumped strength into her voice: *Don't fence me in.*

"Not bad," he said, taking ten dollars of her babysitting money for the gas. "Listen. You going to be around later? You want to get breakfast with me?"

He was blushing, and Portia gave him a smile. It was the same smile her sister and brother gave her when letters arrived from the vocational school reporting that she was failing Office Procedures or had been suspended for smoking.

"Sorry," she said. Shifting into drive, she rolled out to the road on a few bars of "Delta Dawn," the only other country song she knew.

By dawn the rain stopped, and into its place crept thick fog. All through Kentucky and half of Tennessee, Portia had been thinking that with a little more practice she might actually become Wendy, Patty, or Desiree. Or she could slip her mother's diamond watch onto her wrist and be a movie star or the daughter of a British lord. But now, all road signs hidden by fog and her eyes as dry as snake scales, she considered she might simply vanish. She might become the subject of a Sunday night TV movie, the kind her father loved to ridicule and refused to shut off when he was home. *Vanished: The Portia King Story*, the movie would be called, and a 1-800 number and her latest school picture (retouched and much more flattering even if it no longer looked very much like her) would linger on the screen at the end. On the radio a choir sang "All Things Bright and Beautiful." Portia switched it off, leaned forward over the wheel, and wished for a rest stop where she could park, stand, and feel her legs regain their steadiness on still, solid ground.

Instead she heard a rumble, low at first and growing louder. In the rearview mirror she saw two blurred yellow beams. The beams bore down. The sound grew and grew, like tornado winds. For just a second she shut her eyes. The sound whooshed past, instantly fading, and Portia opened her eyes to thick white silence and the Olsons' car still on the road. She thought about Walter, the boy from school. Maybe this was what it had been like for him the moment the cyanide bubbled in his blood: first loss of vision, then sound, then touch.

"December 7, 1941," she said out loud. "Ten-sixty-six. Fourteen hundred and ninety-two."

The living sound was a comfort, and she kept on, reciting everything she'd ever learned. She sang the jingle from an old YMCA commercial: *Learn how to swim but never swim*

alone. There's safety in numbers, don't strike out on your own.
She said, "Cigarettes cause cancer," and wished she had one.
She said, "All roads lead to Prosperity."

That's what her father used to say when she was little and
he came home at the end of every week. Saturday mornings
they'd walk to the town hall, where the two state highways
bump into each other, then pass on by. Sometimes they'd sit
on the stone bench outside the library and watch the cars
and pickups pull up to the Farm and Home, Sparkle Market,
the Hideaway Bar.

"Really," he told her. "All roads do."

When she was little, Portia believed that. She held in her
mind a picture of the United States spread out maplike with
plane, train, and truck routes all pointed towards their small
Ohio town. But when she grew older and found that the
nearest interstate was fifty miles away, the airport farther
yet, she learned the truth: A few roads lead away from
Prosperity; most don't even come close.

Finally at a rest stop she parked, cut the motor, and
stretched out across the front seat. Placing three fingers
above her rib cage, she took deep, slow breaths. It was an
acting exercise she'd learned when her sister, Marcia, won a
leading role in the high school's production of *Oliver!* You
lie on your back, Marcia had told her, find your center, and
then meditate on a peaceful scene.

Portia tried to meditate on the ocean, stretching the borders of her imagination to hold the deep blue waters. She tried to place herself on the sand just above where the waves lap the shore. How different from old, cold Prosperity Florida would be. No railroad tracks, no straight and narrow streets, no slouchy dark houses or boys found dead from cyanide poisoning. All would be new, light, and spacious. Jobs, like lemons and bananas, would grow on trees. If you didn't like one, you could grab yourself another, work right on the beach wearing a bathing suit. Portia concentrated on the ocean, how wide beyond limits it must be. What she kept seeing, though, was more like a postcard, small enough to hold in her hand, a faraway picture of a place someone else had found.

Portia's father once told her he'd wanted to be an actor, serious and revered like Lawrence Olivier. He had the looks, he said, and the talent, not to mention eyes as blue as Sinatra's. Sometimes he'd pull from his dresser an old, leather-bound edition of Shakespeare's plays and, Portia at his feet, he would read for an hour or more. He loved the tragedies best, characters twisted and flawed: the maniacal Iago, the defeated Lear. He told her he'd named her after his favorite Shakespeare heroine, though her mother disagreed. Portia, she said, was the closest she'd let him come to naming his daughter after his favorite car.

Once when he read to Portia from *Richard the Second* in a voice faraway and strange, her mother looked up from her crossword and said, "Stop that. You're scaring her."

He smiled. "'What must the king do now?'" he asked. "'Must he submit?'"

She scowled, and he winked at Portia, whispering, "That's Shakespeare."

Another time he shut the book, peered down at her, and said in a low, grave voice, "You can be anything you want to be. I mean it. Anything at all. All you have to do is imagine."

Portia's mother looked up. "You sound just like some movie," she said. She shook her head and softly laughed, but Portia nodded, very serious, believing everything her father said was just as true as trees. One day he might even say "Surprise!" and reveal the life he'd been keeping from them, one in which his talents were recognized and richly reward- ed, one in which he was everything he had imagined himself to be. A cold draft crept over Portia's ankles. She pulled her scarf over her ears and tried to imagine herself into warmth and sunlight. Then she heard a rap at the window.

An old man wearing a dark hat with fuzzy earflaps peered in.

"You all right?" he asked as she inched down the window.

"Fine," she replied. She searched her mind for a name, a story, to offer him, but she could think of nothing but that postcard ocean and the words *Visit Sunny Florida.*

"I'm just resting," she said.

The man's brows knitted together, but his eyes were mild and kind. He looked concerned, and suddenly, Portia want- ed him to keep looking at her that way. She gripped the door handle, stared up at him with wide-stretched eyes, tried to look like one of the orphans in *Oliver!* or Walter helpless in the back row of her Business Math class. At the very sight, the old man would melt. He'd lead her to the visitors' center, buy her a cup of hot chocolate, ask to hear her story—the true story, not a TV movie, not letting a single lie get by. She'd tell him she missed the man she believed her father once had been, that she herself was dying, rule by rule, in Office Procedures. She'd confess she had only fifteen dollars left, and he'd give her the money to get to Florida so she could waitress or dance until someone identified the latent talent she must surely possess. Or he'd convince her to head back home, earn that A in Office Procedures, whatever he felt was best.

The man said, "Awful chilly out here. You should move along."

Portia nodded.

"Places like this," he said, leaning down close so she could see his teeth, large, clean, and yellowed, "aren't always safe for a girl like you. You never know what kind you might meet."

At that, Portia quickly rolled up the window, and turned the key. The car felt suddenly casket cold, and for a long time it stayed that way. She blasted the heat, but it didn't help. The Olsons' car was starting to whine each time she pressed on the gas. Into Portia's imagination crept everything she'd ever seen on a Sunday night TV movie, and she wished she'd thought about the future enough to have chosen a car registered with AAA.

It was just past Chattanooga, the sky clearing to chalky gray, that she saw the sign: *Nashville, This Exit.* The sign didn't say Nashville was to the west. It didn't say it was more than a hundred miles away. She had a full tank of gas but in her purse only change and her mother's watch. The watch was silver with a delicate band and a spray of diamonds around the timepiece—too elegant and expensive, her mother said, for everyday. Nashville, Portia decided, was just the place to pawn it.

Tennessee flattened out as she headed west, and she found that what those hills had been hiding was nothing, nothing at all. The land was blank—dead fields, dried corn, lightly covered with snow. She blinked, tried to see something on the horizon. *All you have to do is imagine,* her father had said. But all she could imagine was the gas gauge needle sinking lower and lower.

It was nearly noon, and by now, Portia figured, her mother and the Olsons must have gotten together and figured out that her missing daughter and their missing Oldsmobile were linked. Portia pictured the clerk steno lab at the vocational school, her desk empty, the typewriter covered and silent. All around the other girls would be whispering the news like they did the day that Walter died.

"Did you hear about Walter?" a girl had asked her, and at first Portia couldn't picture who he was.

"You know, skinny kid with glasses. Sat in the back in Business Math. His dad owns the antique shop downtown."

Portia nodded, seeing him in the back row, his pale hand gripping a pencil so hard the blue veins stood out, his eyes swimming behind thick lenses.

The girl's voice dropped to a whisper. "He's dead! Early this morning he was cleaning old coins in the store—they use cyanide to do that, you know—and he put some in his Dr Pepper and drank it!"

They were moving down the corridor between pockets of whispering students, and Portia was saying the obligatory oh-my-Gods and you're-kiddings while seeing more clearly Walter's face.

"And that's not all. Get this—" The girl stopped and clutched her arm. "They found him across the counter with his hand on the phone, like he was trying to call for help."

The picture was sharp now: the body sprawled, the hand reaching. Like something out of a play, a movie, a Springsteen song. It was a dramatic exit, a grand performance, and three days later the entire school turned out for Walter's funeral.

"Tragic," Portia's father had said, reading about it in the paper. "Fifteen years old. Imagine that."

Then he looked at Portia. "You know him well?"

She nodded and thought her father looked strangely pleased. Heading towards Nashville, she considered too what he'd say when he learned what she had done. She wondered if he would say, "Stole the Olsons' car. Imagine that." She wondered if he would come home.

When the first houses appeared, the Tennessee sky had turned to fragile blue. It was late afternoon, and in the distance Portia could see the sun half sunk behind the hazy outlines of buildings. From a distance, washed in gold, those buildings looked tall and majestic. She caught her breath, whispered, "Nashville," and wondered if this place and not Florida was her destination after all. Maybe she was bound to become Desiree and sing "Don't Fence Me In," wear rhinestones and spangles and a padded bra. Maybe she would live in one of those golden mansions ahead.

Then she reached the town's edge and saw those buildings up close: not mansions at all, but false fronts giving them the look of height and majesty. She saw crumbling brick, peeling plank boards, a narrowing street lined with Triple-X theaters and crusts of dirty snow pushed up to the curb and melting into the gutter. And then she came to a railroad track and hit the brake. Behind her a horn beeped, but she just sat there. Sat there and thought she might as well have stayed in Prosperity.

The horn beeped again, but it made no difference. When

she pressed her foot to the gas, the Olsons' Oldsmobile sputtered and died.

There was a pawnshop in Nashville a block from where Portia's car ran out of gas. A skinny gray man behind the counter squinted at her mother's diamond watch and shook his head.

"Five bucks," he said.

Portia stared at him. "These are diamonds," she told him.

He chuckled. "Now honey, who told you that?"

She tried again. "Okay. Twenty." Twenty would get her at least to the Georgia line, and Georgia ought to be warm.

"Five," the man said. "Tops. It's not even worth that."

For a moment Portia pictured the watch in its velvet-lined case on her mother's dresser, a five-dollar watch that only looked like more. She wondered what her father had said when he gave it to her. Maybe he'd said, "Only the best for you." Maybe he had quoted something from Shakespeare.

"Ten?" she tried.

This time the man behind the counter didn't reply. He didn't even look up.

Outside, the daylight fading to murky yellow and the lights of the Triple-X theaters flashing, Portia stood at the curb, looked down into a sewer, and pictured herself throwing that watch away. Like an actress on the stage just before the final curtain drops, she'd make a dramatic cry, then let it go. There would be a plink or a splash and it would be gone. She reached down, the watch dangling between thumb and forefinger, and then she remembered Walter. Walter holding a medicine dropper between his thumb and forefinger. Walter deciding to squeeze. She thought of another performance too, of her sister in *Oliver!* and how at the end she died. Every night for a week plus Sunday matinee Marcia died on stage. She did it so well—body limp, voice trembling, slowly fading—that the first time Portia saw her, she gripped her mother's arm tight, and her mother whispered, "It's only a play." Even so, Portia was almost surprised to see Marcia resurrected for the curtain call.

Walter, of course, couldn't be resurrected. He was dead, merely dead, and Portia had had to drive all the way to Nashville just to figure this out.

As she followed the road that led back to Prosperity, the gas tank full and her wallet stuffed with the money her mother had wired, Portia kept her imaginings to the simple and the possible. She would walk through the door and find her father there, his tie askew and his hair disheveled. She would sit him down and tell him what had happened to her and what she had figured out standing on that curb in Nashville, Tennessee. "This isn't a play," she would tell him. "You can't just bow out. Yes, we can be whatever we imagine, and we can imagine that we are a family." Her mother would take a roast from the oven then, and they would all sit down to dinner—Mom, Dad, Marcia, her, and even Bill, home from West Point. She would nod to her father and he would say grace. Her mother would pass around a basket of bread.

But when she arrived, though her father's sedan sat in the drive, only her mother stood in the front hall. She took two steps forward, stopped, and bit her lip.

"The Olsons are expecting you," her mother said. At her sides her arms flapped as if she wasn't quite sure what to do with them. "You'll need to speak to them. But first you better head upstairs now if you want to see your father—"

He was already on his way down. In his hands he gripped not one suitcase but two. Tucked beneath his arm was the leather-bound edition of Shakespeare's plays.

"Oh," he said. He tried to smile, but his eyes squinted as if in bright sunlight. "You're home," he said. Turning to her mother, he added, "See? I told you she would be all right."

Portia said nothing. She stared at him, at that book tucked beneath his arm like a rolled newspaper, at his gray trench coat open with the sash hanging loose. His shoulders were square and straight; there was a cigarette pinched between his lips, and when Portia looks back on that moment, she sees him in a hat with the brim cocked over one eye, though her father never wore a hat. Words like *jaunty* and *debonair* ran through her mind, and as she faced him at the door it came to her that his imagination just wasn't as strong as hers.

"Real dashing, Dad," she said. He looked puzzled, then he grinned. When she didn't say anything else, his smile vanished, and he cleared his throat. He said something about how this was hard for him and in time she would come to understand. Portia turned to her mother. She waited for her to laugh and say, "You sound like some movie." But her mother stood freeze-frame still, her head cocked as if to catch the distant strains of violins, the rustle of women reaching into purses for Kleenex.

Mental

When they called their parents to report that Brian had lost his mind, Dad said, "You're just figuring this out?" Mom said, "Give him time. He'll straighten up."

Mom was on the cordless. Her voice came to them in ocean waves.

"He's a grown man," she said. "He'll pull himself together."

"How's the house?" Dad asked. "Rose, how's the new job?"

Rose and Sherry held the phone between them. Sherry could feel her sister's knuckles harden against her cheek. In anger, Rose's mouth would pinch into a tight bud. Thorn, Dad used to call her. Little Miss Out-of-My-Way. Sherry told him about the house, which he missed like a fourth and favorite child. She told them about Rose's new job. Since the divorce, Rose had worked at a dental center whose slogan was *We Cater to Cowards*.

"There's room for advancement," Sherry explained. "Free classes at Lorain County Community if Rose wants to take advantage."

When Rose looked through the college catalogue, she passed over classes in basic cleaning techniques and diseases of the gums. She remarked on courses called "The Sociology of Anger" and "Writing from Rage."

"The kids," Sherry said, "are really supporting her. They're really chipping in."

Then, unable to come up with a story featuring Rose's two kids chipping in, she reported on a freak April snowstorm that melted instantly into mud. In North Carolina, Mom said, they were enjoying an early spring.

"Except the roof—" Dad said.

"When it rains—" Mom agreed.

"Enough to drive you nuts," Dad concluded.

They were not bad parents. This is what Sherry told Rose when they hung up. They were old. They were tired. They had troubles of their own. With Rose and Sherry, they'd been through plenty, and as for Brian, never mind. They should be given a break. They should enjoy warm sun, shrimp cocktails, daily rounds of golf.

Rose wasn't listening. She dialed Brian's number. She held the phone between them. Brian answered, first ring, in a whisper.

"Is that you?" Brian asked.

"Yes," Rose breathed. "Sherry too."

"You won't believe," Brian said, "what's going on now."

In the movies mental illness is whimsy, a harmless escapade. A naked man gambols through a crowded shopping mall. He splashes through the fountain that's only meant for wishes. Everyone else is clothed, appalled. The audience understands that they're the real mental cases, locked up in lives of convention. Or else crazy is a scene from a late-night horror show, a dim basement world of babble, sounds without sense. It means filth, spittle. Crazy is the very worst that could happen to you. Crazy is obvious too.

This is why, Sherry thinks, it took Rose and her so long to figure out that Brian was bats. (*Bats* was how Rose put it, while Sherry preferred words like *disturbed* and *not quite well.*) Every day he called, sometimes Sherry and sometimes Rose, and told them a story. The story, plausible enough, started a few months before. A local woman, her jealous boyfriend, headlights, high beam, in Brian's driveway late at night. At first it was nothing new. Brian had always been picked on. He was trusting, easy prey. That year there was such a boy in Sherry's seventh-grade social studies class. At lunch the other boys would take him out behind the athletic equipment shed, hang him up by his hood on a peg. Sherry didn't know how they got him back there. If he was dragged, a teacher would have noticed, blown the whistle. Sherry imagined the boys must lure him there with promised friendship, a look at a dirty magazine.

Whenever she lifted Alex down from his peg—he always tried to smile, pretend it was all in good fun—she was reminded of her brother. Brian worked at the Kroger's in Elyria. It was a good job. He had a union card. But some of the other employees, kids, made messes in the aisles. Eggs leapt from their cartons. Jugs of malt syrup mysteriously sprang leaks. Brian, smiling, shrugging, probably suspicious but maybe not wanting to be, went as directed to clean it up. Sure, it broke Sherry's heart. Every day it did. But what could she do? He was a grown man, after all.

Sherry and Rose only worried, at that time, that the jealous boyfriend might own a gun, might really be a nutcase. "Stay away," they advised their brother. "He'll get bored, soon enough."

They didn't wonder, or not out loud, whether there might be more to it, if something—what? legal or not?—had taken place between Brian and this woman. Though he was nearly thirty years old, Sherry believed he must be a virgin.

Sherry lived an hour north, by Cleveland, and had only recently straightened herself out like a stick. No more religion and lost causes. No more living sandal-footed in sagging tents or chaining herself to trees. After five years in the Pacific Northwest she'd returned to an Ohio of shut-down steel mills, abandoned strip malls, and her own reduced expectations. Monday, clean the cat box. Tuesday, water the plants. She followed this schedule as she used to follow her breath. When she called Rose, it was to talk about the kids, the new job. They talked about what it was like for Rose to live back in the old family house. Rose sent monthly rent checks to Mom and Dad, retired in North Carolina and, with the stock market's deep dip, keenly concerned about the state of their finances.

The sisters didn't talk about Brian, not at first. Brian's story grew, still plausible but more alarming. It was as if the story knew that they were getting bored: Rose hugging the phone as she tweezed a sliver from her daughter's thumb; Sherry correcting the weekly quizzes—she could do twenty in one phone call if she didn't say much. Now Brian told them about a rock thrown through his living-room window, a three-in-the-morning shotgun blast, having to do not just with a small-town woman but with money, drugs.

"You should move," Rose advised.

"Come up to Cleveland," Sherry suggested. "You've got vacation coming. Just a week, until this blows over."

Sherry bought another set of sheets, fluffy towels, in case Brian came to stay. She liked this idea of herself: a woman with a clean apartment preparing for a guest; a woman doing her weekly shopping, planning balanced meals, buying meat. These were the things, basic things, Brian had never learned to do. When bills came, he dropped them, unopened, on his living-room floor. They crunched under foot like autumn leaves. He said the bills were too difficult to read. The letters shivered, he said, and would not stay still. His car was repossessed, the telephone disconnected. He called Sherry and Rose from the Sohio station. He said his phone had been tapped anyhow, his car rigged to explode.

"He's mental," Rose said. "Certifiable."

"Don't say that," Sherry replied. She thought of the names Dad used to call them: Thorn, Airy, Brainless. "Don't call them that," Mom would object. "They'll turn out that way."

"Bonkers," Rose continued. "Off his rocker, nuts."

"All right," Sherry had finally agreed. "So what do we do now?"

They had never been as Sherry imagined other siblings to be. They didn't get together as children to put on plays with Rose, the oldest, bossing them about until Brian or Sherry cried "No fair!" and "I quit!" On long car trips they hadn't fought over backseat territory. At one window Sherry sat reading about the lives of martyrs. She wished she shared the name of a saint instead of being named for a before-dinner drink. At the other window Rose hunched over her hands. With a needle she pricked their scabby backs until she bled *R+C 4-ever.* In between, according to his age, sat Brian. He played silent games of rock, scissors, paper. Sometimes his left hand won and sometimes his right.

"Not really a game you can play by yourself," Dad would remark, eyeing him in the rearview mirror. "Hey, Brainless, did you hear me?" Brian, unperturbed, went on or switched to a new game: Twenty Questions, I Spy.

Such were the memories Rose said they should spread before the white-jacketed professionals to whom they would bring their brother. Sherry wasn't convinced this was a course they should pursue, especially not now that she'd finally resolved to live by her parents' motto that if you don't look trouble straight in the eye, it will, eventually, go away. Shouldn't she and Rose just give Brian time? Shouldn't they avoid doing anything rash? Lately this image had stuck itself to Sherry's brain: their brother heel-dragged down a narrowing corridor, twisting around to raise an accusing finger except his arms are straitjacketed, bound. She tried to meditate on the idea of trained professionals with explanatory power. The image grew: Brian cast into a damp dungeon room, his head in a helmet, his temples wired.

"That's the movies," Rose snapped. "Watch it, or you'll be telling stories too."

Rose, it turned out, was born to direct. Lunch first, she said. Glasses of wine all around. She wanted to put Brian in a happy haze. She selected a shopping-mall restaurant, two exits from the hospital. Brian sat across from them in the booth. Since it had no pictures, Sherry and Rose read the menu to him. What about the grilled chicken breast with tangy cilantro and lime? they asked him. How about the fiesta nachos supreme? Brian was neatly dressed in a striped jersey and new jeans. His hair was combed; his teeth appeared to have been brushed. Sherry wasn't sure if he knew where they were headed, but he seemed to want to make a good impression. The night before he'd called Rose and instead of telling her the story, he asked if he could come over and do some wash.

Rose elbowed Sherry and indicated a table of women nearby. They wore pretty flowered dresses and aerobic-training shoes. They gave Brian flirty smiles. Brian smiled back. He even winked. It was the sort of moment that gave Sherry hope. It brought second thoughts to roost on the table beside Brian's untouched glass of wine. Everything he'd told them, after all, could be true. Even if it involved drug lords, police scams, a videotaped sex scandal, well, didn't they hear about such things on the nightly news, read about them in the newspaper section called "Around the World"? Maybe there was still the chance Brian could learn to read, manage his money, marry a pretty girl.

Then Brian turned back and began to speak. Like flighty birds the second thoughts took off. Brian wasn't telling the story. The story was telling him. When it bumped into something new, it reached out, folded the new thing in. The secretaries, he said, were undercover feds. They'd been sent to this restaurant to spy.

"Yes," Rose said, though Brian didn't seem to hear. The story absorbed all of his concentration.

"So hard," Rose said, "what you're going through."

Beneath the table she gave Sherry a kick, harder than she needed to.

"So stressful—" Sherry added.

"Yes," Rose agreed. "That's why we're going to see some-one—"

"Someone to talk to—"

"Get some advice—"

"Figure this thing out—"

"So hard—"

"What you're going through."

They spoke carefully. They sifted for each word like a precious gem. They didn't want to look the wrong way, say the wrong thing, end up inside the story too. We're your sisters. We're your friends. You can trust us. We mean you no harm. Sherry thought of Alex in the school yard, the other boys luring him out behind the shed. Then she reminded herself that, of course, this was different.

"They'll never look for you here," Rose said when they turned onto the hospital drive. In the front seat Brian had turned suddenly stiff. He seemed to sniff the air. When he twisted around, the shoulder strap caught him at the neck.

"They'll never dream," Sherry added.

"You'll be safe," they said.

But from that moment Sherry couldn't help it. She saw them on a movie screen. A slow-motion camera followed them out of the car, up the walk, and into the lobby, where they introduced Brian to a young woman who said she would be handling his intake. The woman was very small, very young, dressed in gray slacks and a pink blouse, a stethoscope draped casually around her neck like a scarf.

Her name tag said she was Roxanne, nothing so formal as a last name or the M.D. it turned out she was. She looked like a pixie, a friendly elf. Brian smiled at her. He began to tell her the story. There were parts to this story Sherry had not heard before. In these parts, Brian was a live-action hero. Yes, he told Roxanne. Oh, yes, he had guns—a Luger, an Uzi, an AK-47.

"Jesus," Rose said, then pinched her lips so she wouldn't say more.

"I see," Roxanne said. "Anything else?"

No, Brian, no! This is what Sherry imagined the movie audience, who knew better, shouting out. *Run, Brian, run!* Their hero had talked himself into a trap. Roxanne's face showed no surprise. She must have heard such stories before or read about people like Brian in her medical-school text-books. She asked Brian if he'd ever fired his guns—when and at what and how many times? The movie audience sat back. They relaxed their grip on the armrests, resigned themselves to what would happen next.

A few minutes later when Rose and Sherry made their exit, instructed to call first before returning for visiting hours, Sherry imagined the audience hissing, throwing pop-corn at their retreating backs. "No fair!" she wanted to turn around and shout. "What would you do?" In this movie they were the villains, the wicked sisters; they were judged. "You try having him for a brother. You see what it's like."

"I can't believe we did that," Rose said. They were back on

the highway, heading home. The traffic was thick and snarled. They inched by an electronic sign that said *Expect Minor Delays.* From the radio came news headlines that sounded a lot like Brian's stories.

Sherry was about to agree. She couldn't believe they'd done it either or that it had gone so fast. She wasn't sure what she'd expected—a judge, at least, a courtroom drama that ended with the thud of a gavel, then heavy doors giving way to the symbolism of sunlight, making clear to everyone that this time Sherry was exactly right to walk away. Then she realized Rose was smiling, happily.

"We did it," Rose said. "He liked Roxanne so much, he practically wanted to stay."

Practically. Not quite.

"Where are you going?" Brian had asked when Roxanne ushered them out of the interview room. The room had two doors, one leading back to the lobby and the other some-place else.

"We're just going to the Coke machine," Rose had lied.

"Yes," Sherry said. "You want one too?"

"Mountain Dew," Brian replied.

But then, a second later, he'd cried out, "No! Wait!"

At the door Sherry and Rose both stopped dead. They turned.

"Make that a Sprite," Brian said.

In the end there was nothing for them to sign and no opportunity to unpack their stories of childhood. Roxanne had listened to Brian for five minutes, and that, she said, was enough. In Brian's case, Roxanne had added, talking was the problem, not the cure.

Brian's room was like any hospital room, shoe-box spare. There was a bed, standard-issue, and a vinyl-seated chair. Sherry noticed the absence of curtains and shades, the tiny closet without hangers. Brian's sneakers, laces removed, were tucked within. The first night they came to visit, he stayed on the bed, facing them, his knees drawn up to his chin. He said he was bored, there was nothing to do. He rocked himself gently, and Sherry wished he wouldn't. He looked like a small child. He looked like he was about to suck his thumb. Rose went down to the nurses' station to see about a TV. Brian went back to the story. They'd locked him up so he couldn't speak the truth. They'd taken his belt, replaced his shoes with soft rubber-studded socks. Out of the blue he said that this was the very worst. He was afraid to stand lest his pants fall down. He hated the padded sound of his slippered feet. Sherry could barely understand him. His words gummed together.

"Humiliated," he said. "They wanted to humiliate me, and that's what they've done."

Sherry waited, stomach tight, for him to speak her name. Instead he told her that every two hours they called him down the hall, handed him a pleated paper cup full of pills, then checked under his tongue to make sure he'd swallowed.

"Humiliated," he said. "That's what I am."

He went back to the very beginning. A local woman, her jealous boyfriend. The story was so familiar now, so dull. Sometimes Brian paused, rewound, went back to retrieve a missed detail. This story would take all night. Sherry imagined the movie audience growing restless, tiptoeing out for more popcorn and a smoke.

"There's a TV," Rose announced. "It's across the hall, in the common room."

"Oh, right," Brian said. "Like I'm going to sit over there with the crazies."

He glanced at them and added that someone, he wasn't sure yet who, had been planted on this ward, a hired gun.

"We know you believe that," Rose said, gently. "And we want you to know that while we love you, we don't share your belief."

She gave Sherry a look, and Sherry added, "We know it seems real to you." Sherry shrugged and tried to smile. "It just isn't real to us."

This was what they'd been instructed to say. They were to point out, quietly and without judgment, their alternative view of reality. They were to act as if either version could be true, even though it was their version, not his, that allowed them to come and go, hang onto their shoelaces and belts. The glass door to Brian's ward was kept locked. When Rose and Sherry were ready to leave, they paused at the nurses' station. Someone would take a good look at them, then buzz them out. They'd also been instructed to visit Brian's house, search for guns, videotapes, and maybe bones, the remains of the small-town woman.

"In every delusion," Roxanne said, "there is a grain of truth."

She didn't actually tell them to search for bones. This is just what Sherry imagined, what seemed to be implied.

"It's chemistry," Rose told Mom and Dad. "It has nothing to do with toilet-training, birth order, or dreams."

"You could have called him anything," she told Dad. "It wouldn't have made any difference."

They'd reached Mom and Dad on their cell phone. Their parents were on their way back from a fish place that offered two-for-one dinners on Tuesday nights if you arrived before five and showed your AARP or AAA card. Sometimes their voices gave way to static. They came and went. Mom was sorry for believing all these years that Brian's problems were all in his head. Dad said what was done was done and they should look to the future, listen to Brian's doctors. Rose said the doctors would treat Brian with lithium.

"Everyone these days is on it," Rose added, voice bright. "Artists, physicists, real geniuses."

Mom, Dad, and Rose all speculated about what Brian's diagnosis would be. They were hoping for manic-depression. Mom said she would check out some books. Dad said he would send Brian a beeper watch to remind him to take his meds. He used the word meds easily. Meds were what he took for his heart and hip. Sherry and Rose didn't mention that Brian had been deemed a potential threat to himself or others. Their parents were old, tired, and perpetually dismayed to find that their retirement savings weren't nearly enough. Why worry them more?

"So he'll be there a couple of days," Rose said.

"Just until they get the medication right," Sherry added.

That week Sherry would also check out books about Mozart and Virginia Woolf. Sometimes she could forget to wonder whether Brian really fit with such tales of mad brilliance. The books made her shiver, like those she'd read as a child about the lives of martyrs and saints. She felt close to something great and misunderstood. These were stories, unlike the one of basement bones, she could live with.

When Brian didn't respond to lithium, the doctors tried mood-adjusters, antipsychotics, different combinations of each. The antipsychotics made Brian's hands shake, but he seemed to tell the story a little less. When Sherry and Rose visited, they found him across the hall, watching TV. The nurses reported that he had voluntarily attended the morning session of group therapy. In group therapy, Brian said, they wrote down what they admired about each other. He showed Sherry and Rose the pieces of paper he'd collected in his pocket. He read them aloud, sounding out each syllable. *Brian cares about how you are. Brian is very smart.* He said these were the nicest things anyone had ever said about him.

Sherry thought of the progress reports Brian used to bring home from school: *Brian doesn't do his work, he doesn't pay attention, he would do better if he would just apply himself.* At Kroger's, she and Rose had recently learned, he was on probation for showing up late. Since his car had been repossessed, he'd been riding buses to work, reversing the numbers, ending up on a wrong route. Sherry hadn't known about any of this because whenever he'd called, his stories so rambling and confused, she'd barely listened: *Ummm-hmmm. Oh no. Well, that's too bad.* Maybe, Sherry thought now, Brian didn't want to be a live-action hero. Maybe, like anyone, he just wanted to be noticed, appreciated, liked. A little attention, a kindly word—forget the meds—maybe this was all it would take.

"Hey," Rose said, chucking his knee. "It sounds like you're making friends."

Brian ducked his head and agreed. The other patients were all right, just checking in for a mental tune-up. He said most checked in at least once a year.

Rose's mouth pinched up tight. "Really," she said.

"So I've figured out," Brian continued, "that none of them is the one."

"The one?" Sherry asked.

"The one who's out to get me."

This was Brian's fifth day in the hospital. All week Rose had been spending a fortune, as she put it, on sitters for the kids. Sherry was anxious to get home too. She'd been told her students loved their substitute. Her cats didn't miss her at all. The movie audience had long since gone home. This story had no action, no drama. It was simply dragging on.

On the next visit, Brian told them he was coming up with a list of goals. He was going to be on time for work. He was going to clean his house and get his car back.

"That's terrific," Rose said. "Is there anything we can do to help?"

Yes, Brian replied. Could they co-sign for his car and find him a trustworthy mechanic—someone from out of town or maybe out of state—to check out the engine, make sure it hid no bombs? Rose glared at him. Sherry started to say, "We know it's real to you," but Rose broke in, "Jesus, Brian, do you have any idea what this place costs? Do you even know the word *co-pay?* Couldn't you at least pretend to be sane?"

Every day Roxanne asked them if they'd stopped by Brian's house. No, Rose said. They hadn't had time.

"You need to make time. Like I said, in every delusion—"

"Maybe," Rose said to Sherry that night, "Brian will meet someone, fall in love. Not with another patient, of course, but maybe a nurse or even Roxanne."

Sherry had once seen a movie about a man who was mental but talented too. He could paint or compose music. A capable, well-off woman fell for him, head over heels. Yes, he was difficult but in the way that three-year-olds are difficult, delightful too. They lived outrageously ever after. The audience was envious of their love. Maybe, Sherry thought, Brian's story could turn into one about love. Then she remembered Denise, a woman who once said she loved Brian. She had been smart, capable, majoring in pre-med, planning to become a pediatrician. She was better than a movie star, the answer to their prayers. Except Brian had refused to love her back. Denise, he declared, had a hairy upper lip. This was the problem with Brian. On the surface he appeared pleasant, easy, manageable. But underneath was something surprisingly hard and stubborn. This was the problem: he had his own ideas.

Two days later Roxanne told them that in the morning, Brian would be going home. By noon at the latest, they should come and pick him up.

"But he's still telling the story," Rose said.

"Not as much," Roxanne replied. "Not as often."

"But he isn't all better," Sherry protested.

Roxanne placed a hand on her shoulder. She said, "This is better. This is what better looks like."

They were standing on the other side of the glass door, the side that meant you could be in this hospital for any reason—to have your gallbladder removed or visit your dying grandmother. Through the glass Sherry watched Brian shuffle out of his room. Maybe if he'd been on her side of the door, she would have called it walking. But what she saw was Brian shuffling, one hand hitching up the waist to his pants.

He waved at her. She waved back and thought he looked like someone who belonged there.

"Do you think," Sherry asked, "Brian will meet someone?"

"Get a clue," Rose replied.

She added, "He just needs to straighten up."

Rose had spent that morning looking at college catalogues—not from Lorain County Community but from what she called real colleges, universities. She'd filled out a financial aid questionnaire and crowed to see that she likely qualified.

"Like I've always said, when life gives you cherries—"

"Lemons," Sherry corrected.

"Cherries, lemons, whatever."

They were on their way up the walk to Brian's house. They would get things in order, poke around, search for the grain of truth. Inside was not as bad as Sherry had imagined. The refrigerator was empty, nothing there to turn moldy or sour. No ghastly smell arose from the basement. It was bare except for a toppled three-legged chair and a rotting Ouija board that Brian, for some reason, had always hung onto.

"Maybe we should take it out," Sherry suggested. "Ask it what the future holds." She was only half-joking. She imagined the Ouija board lighting up like a road sign: *Expect Minor Delays.*

Rose snorted, heading back up the stairs. That morning as she flipped through the college catalogues, she'd scoffed at majors in the pillow-soft liberal arts. She would go after something tangible, real like biochemistry or industrial engineering. Upstairs they raked up the bills, opened the shades, sneezed in the little clouds of dust. Sherry ignored the videotapes stacked around the TV set. She thought maybe Rose hadn't seen them. When they found the gun, it was only Dad's old hunting rifle, propped behind the coat tree by the door. Rose emptied out the bullets. In Brian's neighborhood of tiny rented bungalows and duplexes lived young families and retired couples. Little kids rode Big Wheels on the sidewalks. Sherry noticed how close they came to Brian's door, how little aim it would take. A potential threat to himself or others. It could be true.

They took the gun out to the car, and a neighbor called to them, "Everything all right in there?"

The neighbor was an elderly man. He sat in a low chair on a small front porch. The day was clear, cool, and promising spring.

"Anything going on I should know about?"

"Everything's fine," Sherry called back. She hesitated. "Why do you ask?"

The man shrugged. "It just occurred to me that all of a sudden the news vans could roll in, and I'd be saying to some reporter, 'He was always such a quiet boy. He never caused any trouble before.'"

He pointed to Rose's hands. "And isn't that a gun you're carrying?"

"Ignore him," Rose said to Sherry under her breath. "He's just some nut."

Later Sherry will find it strange, or maybe predictable, how they each tell this story in a different way. In these stories Brian is almost a minor character, or the catalyst for their individual revelations. Rose, for instance, tells the story of how during this troubled time (she now prefers words like *troubled, disturbed, not quite well*) she discovered she was a person of strength and capability. She did go to college while working full-time and raising her children admirably. She graduated *cum laude* and became the subject of an alumni magazine cover story. She is a role model, an inspiration.

It was also at this time that Mom found her voice. She visits book clubs, junior leagues; she talks about mental illness, brain biology, the need for compassion and better prescription drug coverage. She receives phone calls, letters, cards of thanks. Dad has joined a group of men who have recently discovered they have feelings. They go on weekend retreats, talk about how their own fathers let them down, and about how this isn't any excuse. He doesn't get worked up, not anymore, about personal finances or the condition of their roof. He's put such matters in their place.

The stories they tell are different but the message is the

same: They have learned and grown and are all getting better. When their stories bump into certain stubborn facts—Brian never gets a diagnosis, the medications make him soft and slow—they make the facts fit or else leave them out. This is not so bad, Sherry believes. It could have been much worse.

Brian alone has no story to tell. He is much more manageable now that he no longer thinks of himself as a live-action hero and no one regards him as a grown-up man.

After Rose packed the gun into the trunk, she turned to Sherry. They should stop by Kroger's, she said, and pick up milk, toilet paper, eggs. They should drop Brian's prescriptions at the pharmacy to be ready when they returned. They should also stop by the county offices, make an appointment with a social worker and find out if Brian qualified for SSI. Rose said she hoped Sherry wasn't thinking of heading back to Cleveland, dumping Brian on her. Sherry winced. These days she seemed to have no control over what popped into her head, no ability to evaluate and discern. She could see herself picking up the phone, dialing Brian's number, but only when she was certain no one was home. She could hear herself saying to Rose, "Look, I have to deal with kids all day. What more do you want from me?" It wasn't an idea of herself she especially liked, not the kind of thing she'd dreamed about back when she believed she might be persecuted for her beliefs or could save a tree. But it seemed plausible, possibly true.

Then Rose announced, "Back inside. One more thing we have to do."

"No," Sherry said. "So he likes movies, so what."

"Come on," Rose said, firmly.

The tapes, maybe a dozen of them, were stacked around the TV. The VCR's red light had winked at them as they'd cleaned, gathered, and emptied out the gun.

"Don't," Sherry said. Rose moved toward the TV. Sherry shut her eyes. She imagined all kinds of things. The old man would say he knew it, he'd had a funny feeling. Brian would make the news.

"Look," Rose said. "Open your eyes. It's not what you think."

Sherry looked, and then they checked a second videotape and a third. They were all the same. They were episodes of *Reading Rainbow* and *Sesame Street*. When Brian was in school, they'd sent him to specialists, and he'd come back talking like a specialist. "Reading," he'd say, "is a process of prediction and surprise. You predict what kind of story this will be, then check to see if what's there really fits." Still, he couldn't get through a story about Dick and Jane without saying he needed to throw up. Years later, he was still trying. Today was being brought to them by the letter L. There was a song about listening, then a lesson about the difference between here and there. Rose put a hand to her mouth, feigned coughing, and then she just let go. Sherry too.

"L is for loony," Rose gasped. She laughed harder.

"For lithium," Sherry said. They howled. Sherry glanced at her watch.

"L is for late."

"In a minute," Rose replied. "I can't believe Brian watches these things. It's so sad."

At that, they laughed again. They laughed like crazy. It was such a relief. It felt so good. They watched another episode and another after that. They giggled and shook their heads. Sherry assured Rose she would do her part. Really, when she thought about it, Brian was so vulnerable and sweet. Rose said she was glad Sherry felt that way and wasn't it funny how Brian was drawing them all so close.

When Sherry offers her version of the story, she always concludes, "So this was what better looked like. This was the best we could do." She comes to this conclusion, insists on it, even though she knows there's at least one scene she can't make fit: Brian at the door with his shoes laced up. This is at the end of his first time in the hospital or his second or third. He bobs up on his toes, peers through the glass, looks back at a nurse. The nurse is thinking about transferring to a different ward, one where people actually get well, or maybe where they don't and so their delusions are something to encourage and bless. *Yes, there's a heaven. Look, there's the pearly gates.* The young man bobs up, peers out, glances back at the clock.

"They're coming," he says. "They're on their way."

Running to Ethiopia

"Your sister is searching for her identity," Mom said. "That's natural. That's okay."

She paused. "So long as your father doesn't find out."

I sat at the kitchen table and pretended to be absorbed in a find-a-word. Pretended because, in fact, I was spying through the sliding-glass door on Al with her boyfriend, Billy. They sat on the patio swing, not a breath of space between them, their heads touching. Al's hair was long, thick, and dark, and it hung like a heavy curtain so I couldn't see her face. But I could see Billy with his cow-brown eyes fixed on Al. He was a slight boy with hands that seemed too big for the rest of him. He took Al's arm, turned it to the soft underside, and ran one finger from her elbow to wrist and back. Slowly and rhythmically he stroked, raising goose bumps on my own arms. The find-a-word was called "What Little Girls Are Made Of," and barely glancing down, I circled the easy horizontals: *Frocks. Frills. Smiles. Curls.*

"It's hormones that are making her impossible," Mom said. "We shouldn't take it personally."

I nodded, circled *sugar-and-spice,* and imagined Billy's hot breath on my cheek. Earlier when he ambled through the house, all crooked loose limbs like the stick figures Al and I used to draw, he'd mumbled "Hi" to Mom but his eyes slid over me. Mom managed only the faintest company smile. Her eyes followed him, narrowing, as if he might suddenly reach out and swipe the good silver we didn't even own.

Now Mom stooped over the dishwasher, loading lunch plates. I watched a line of sweat slip down her cheek. The heat hushed up the afternoon, the only sounds the light clatter of dishes and creak-creak of the patio swing.

"I'm sure he's a nice boy. It's just he never has anything to say."

She wasn't expecting me to reply. She simply needed someone to talk to, and now that Al had Billy, this meant me. I learned that Mrs. O'Connell next door took Valium and that Mom had been trying to talk my father into having a vasectomy. She didn't want to end up like Mrs. Reardon down the street, practicing rhythm with seven-and-a-half kids to show for it. As Mom talked, the swing's steady creak crawled like ants up my spine. Then it stopped. I looked up. Mom did too, bent over the dishwasher, a plate between two fingers. We listened, and the silence deepened until it seemed bottomless, like the quarry where the more daring boys went to swim and sometimes drowned.

"Are they still on the patio?" Mom asked.

From behind the kitchen counter she couldn't see as I did, through the sliding-glass door, what was happening. She had to trust me to tell her.

I nodded.

"What are they doing?"

They were kissing. I could see Billy's finger still trailing the tender side of Al's arm. He made long and lazy circles.

"They're talking," I replied.

Mom shut the dishwasher door and reached up to the cupboard. The line between her blouse and shorts parted, showing dimpled stomach and the long jerky scar I would later learn meant she'd had Al and me by caesarian. It was the end of the month, a Tuna Helper night, and I could picture how it would be later when Dad came home. Since she'd turned fifteen, Al hated tuna and food of almost any kind. At supper she would refuse to appear, and Mom would explain, "She's up in bed. You know. A woman's thing." Dad apparently knew little about menstrual cycles and accepted without question that Al could suffer cramps at least three nights a week.

"Quiet boy," he'd remarked the one time Billy came to supper and managed to choke down nothing more than a dinner roll. He hadn't seen, as I had, Billy's hand beneath the table, tickling Al's thigh. Every time I got up from the table—for the margarine, the pepper, more milk, a clean fork—I had a clear view. He was writing letters into her skin.

I watched his finger trace twice the sensuous curves of an *s: k-i-s-s*. He paused for the reward of Al's smile, then moved on to what Al later told me was *w-a-n-t-y-o-u-b-a-d*. He had to do that last one three times before Al's face bloomed. I didn't say a word. Without ever being told, I knew we weren't to tell Dad anything of importance. When he came through the door at five-fifteen, we met him like a guest with polite smiles, soft greetings, the table set for supper.

"Things are shaky at the office," Mom would tell us. "Pink slips, layoffs. Your dad needs some peace and quiet."

I'd nod, seal my lips, and even Al would tread lightly when he was around; her bedroom door whispered instead of slammed. Up and down the block, for-sale signs dotted overgrown lawns. Half a dozen houses stood empty. These were the houses in which my mother used to sit on hot slow summer afternoons, talking with women her own age about vasectomies while I joined a swarm of kids in sweaty games of hide-and-seek. Evenings over the split-rail fences, the fathers would swap facts about fertilizer. Now when Dad spotted a neighbor pushing his lawnmower too, he'd raise a hand, then fix his eyes on his grass-stained shoes. Sometimes when Mom was talking to me, she would stop mid-sentence, say, "What am I doing? Look at who I'm talking to." Then she would shrug. "I guess it's better than talking to myself."

After supper Dad always mixed himself an Old Fashioned and changed the channel to Walter Cronkite. By his recliner in the den, I'd sit quiet, suck on bourbon-soaked oranges, and listen to the way it was: *inflation, communists, Roe v. Wade,* words that made Dad mutter, "The whole world is going to pot, do you realize that, Cassie?" I'd nod, watch the greeny flashes of rifle-waving men who were sometimes called soldiers and sometimes called guerrillas, and try to picture a whole world going to pot. The only signs I saw were the raggedy lawns and the high-pitched whistle that occasionally sounded through the neighborhood. The whistle came from the women's prison—reformatory, it was called—that edged our subdivision. No fence surrounded it and no guards patrolled. The women were on the honor system, so Dad said, and when one shrugged off honor and ran, the whistle sounded every ten minutes, for one long minute, until she was caught.

Mom pulled a skillet from under the stove and switched the range light on. Billy hiked his hand up Al's thigh and then cupped her crotch. I blinked, looked again, and felt a prickly red spread over my face and neck.

"What are they talking about?" Mom asked. "Not that I'm snooping. I just want to stay in touch."

"Algebra," I answered. Nothing else came to mind. The swing rocked once more, and Billy's hand stayed put. I watched it wriggle between Al's thighs like a caterpillar in the curled nest of a leaf.

That night the whistle sounded. Low, close to the ground at first, it rose and spread like a flapping sheet. Across the hall Al was awake and waiting. Nights when the whistle blew were the only times she let me come near, as if this were one childhood habit she forgot, on turning fifteen, to break. She drew back the covers and pulled me in. With a sleepy hand, she stroked my hair and murmured, "'Sokay, 'Sokay. Don't be scared. 'Sokay."

Down the hall a bedspring groaned and feet hit the carpet. Dad always double-checked the locks when a woman got loose, then slept on the couch in the den. Past Al's door and down the stairs his slippers shuffled, pausing as he jiggled the front doorknob.

"'Sokay," Al whispered. "They aren't bad women. They won't hurt you."

The whistle dropped and my body went stiff. Against me Al did the same, and we waited, very quiet, listening to the crickets and Dad below and for the whistle to sound again.

"Al?" I whispered.

"Alexandra," she said.

"How many of them are there?"

"Three this time, I think."

Like a bedtime story, Al would tell me how many women had run away. She made up names for them and histories, and it was never their fault they were in jail. They'd bounced checks to buy food for hungry children. They'd turned knives into the hearts of men who attacked them. For as long as the whistle sounded, she'd tell me where the women were and where they were running.

"They're heading down Collins Avenue," she said, and I could see it: three women in prison-blue smocks and baggy pants, one with pale arms shimmering in the streetlights, the others with faces brown and coffee-black—colors that never appeared in our subdivision but that I'd seen in the fields outside the reformatory, hunched over rows of lettuce and beans. I saw those three women as if they were right outside Al's window. They ran barefoot, panting, but not tiring, not yet. The whistle had sounded again.

"There's a car waiting," Al told me. "They're getting onto the highway. They're heading for Columbus."

She turned quiet then, as if trying to hear the rumble of the getaway car. The whistle rose moon-high. It trembled like the wails of a thousand starving babies. Against me I could feel the hard thinness of Al's body and the strange soft bumps of her new breasts. Then the whistle dropped. It bird-dived back to earth, thinned to nothing more than vibration, a slight disturbance of the atmosphere, like the unhappy whispers I'd sometimes hear from Mom and Dad's room late at night.

"Al?" I whispered. "Did they get them?"

"Alexandra," she said. "No."

"Where are they going?"

"To Ethiopia," she replied.

Every time she made up someplace new—someplace strange and thrilling and very far from the flat dull middle of Ohio: Thailand, China, India, France. Much later, a grown woman, I would lie half-awake in a marriage that was thank-fully brief. I would tell myself stories of the places I could go.

"How do you get to Ethiopia?" I asked.

Al used my back as a map and charted with her finger their path: from Columbus they would drive to Indian-apolis, Des Moines, then Boulder. They'd travel over moun-tains, chug through desert, all the way to L.A. I'd never been farther than the Indiana border, but I could imagine: wide blue ocean, dancing sunfish, the boat the women would board and sail all by themselves to the Orient.

"But then," I asked, "how will they go?"

"By camel," Al answered.

The dream of it came easy to me, a rolling camel ride over desert dunes. I drifted towards sleep with Al's voice fuzzy in my ears, her fingers like tiny camel toes trotting over my back. Then I felt a finger-flick sharp on my back of my neck.

"It's over," Al said. "Go back to your room."

Al lay on her back with her hair spread like a fan over the pillow, her hands tucked beneath. She stared at the ceiling, her eyes hard stone. I stood beside her and shifted my weight. The carpet felt rough beneath my bare feet. Maybe the whis-tle would rise one more time. Sometimes it lasted all night.

"Go on," she said. "You've got a bed of your own."

As I scuttled across the hall, Mom called, "Cassie? Al?"

"It's me," I answered, and she said, "All right. Go back to bed. Go to sleep."

But back in bed I tried to imagine what must have happened next: three hands-behind-the-back bodies folded into a flashing-light cruiser, a dungeon dug deep into the clay beneath the reformatory. I could see it. The dungeon floor would be cold and slick and scattered with picked-clean bones, like the thrillers I'd seen on late-night TV. The thought of it made my pulse skip, and outside my door I heard a ghost-rustle of sound. I hung onto my breath, waited until only the crickets filled my ears, then crept back across the hall.

"Al? Alexandra?"

This time she didn't answer. This time she wasn't there.

By July humidity roofed the sky in cinderblock gray. I stayed at the kitchen table and did every find-a-word I could find by the Kroger checkout. I imagined I was getting remarkably good and there would be a national, even world-wide, competition I could win, an eleven-year-old word-finding wonder. From the kitchen Mom talked in tune with the humming fan. She said Mrs. O'Connell next door was treating herself to evening cocktails with her Valium, and Dad still went grim at the idea of a vasectomy. Lydia Herschel, she'd heard, had taken her daughter to Columbus for a D-and-C, which of course was just a cover-up word for abortion; why else drive all the way to Columbus?

Rumor was, too, the state would surround the reform-atory with electrified barbed wire, twelve feet high. The whistle sounded at least one night a week and once in the plain bright middle of the day.

"They say the women are getting worse," Mom told me. "They say they're in for doing drugs."

She paused. "Though if that's such a crime, there's a lot in this neighborhood that should be behind bars."

Then she added, "Where's Al?"

On the patio swing Al sat pressed to Billy, their heads nestled like small birds. Sweat ringed Billy's arms and neck, but Al, her body powdered and her pits Soft-and-Dried, looked cool as alabaster each day after rainless day. The grass faded to dusty brown, and then it died, leaving widening patches of dirt that made Dad's shoulders slump whenever he looked out back.

"So how are things?" he'd ask me.

"Good," I'd reply. "Fine."

I'd dig a bare toe into the shag carpet.

"Hot," I'd add.

"Yes, hot," he'd say and stare through the sliding-glass door at the yard, his face slack, as if the sight of dead grass made him very sad.

Meanwhile, Billy had gotten himself a hobby, perhaps so he'd have something to say those times when Mom blocked the path between the front door and back, smiled at him, and said, "So Billy, how are you?"

"I've started collecting cacti," he told her. "I belong to a national club of collectors. I'm the only one in the state of Ohio."

He said this last part a little regretfully, as if the state of

Ohio lacked something vital. I'd never heard of cacti and pictured a strange prehistoric bird with a ropey neck and buzzard head. That made Al snort.

"Cacti," she told me, "is plural for cactus."

"It's probably a good hobby for a boy like Billy," Mom observed. "An esteem-builder. I mean, how could you kill a cactus?"

She stood in the kitchen framed in the space between the formica countertop and the cupboards overhead, just a torso, neck, and partial view of her face, cut off at the eyebrows.

"Are Billy and Al still on the patio?" she asked, and I shook my head, my face suddenly prickly and my thighs uncomfortably damp, pressed together tight as a sealed jar. At that moment I'd looked out to see the swing creak vacant and the door to the backyard shed seal shut.

"They went for a walk around the block," I said.

"Awful hot for a walk," Mom observed, then went back to her work. She scrubbed, vacuumed, sprayed, and swept, but cobwebs still spread in hidden places and something smelly seeped up through the basement rec room carpet. Saying the whole house stank, Al refused to come downstairs even for breakfast, and when she did finally appear in the kitchen, Mom offered her baskets of clean folded laundry. Sometimes Mom paused at the kitchen table and pressed a dishwater-damp hand to my cheek. Was I ill? she wanted to know. Had the whistle troubled my sleep? Or was I just lonely without Al? She reminded me Al was only going through a phase and it was hormones making her act this way.

"They'll break up," she said. "Al will find somebody new."

I shrugged and stuck my eyes back on the find-a-word. This one was called "Where You Live," and I circled *barracks, bungalow, brownstone* with record speed, then asked Mom what "cloister" meant.

"It's a place where women stay," she said. "Religious women. Nuns."

I nodded, circled *cloister,* and went on to *condominium,* thinking about the Catholic church out by the Kroger's. Before Billy came along, Al and I would bike to the cemetery beside the church, practice lying cold, straight, and still, and then jump up, whoop and holler, just to relish the living sound of our voices. Or Al would take me to the field edging the reformatory, where we'd play women in prison. I'd bend my back and pretend-hoe the grass until I heard Al's bird-call signal. Then we'd take off running as if our lives depended on it.

"Wild Indians," Mom called us, shaking her head at our dirt-streaked bodies, our tangled hair. "A couple of savages." Frowning briefly, she'd add, "Get cleaned up. Hurry now. Your father'll be home any minute."

Now Al stayed cleaned up from morning to night on the expectation Billy would stop by, his shirt soaked from the bike ride, his face red as the peppers ripening on the kitchen counter. Late at night I'd hear footfalls too soft for Dad's on the stairs, then the barely there sound of the sliding-glass door murmuring open and shut. If I turned to the window and parted the curtains to the backyard shed, I knew what I would see. Instead, I imagined something else: Al alone, crossing the field dividing us from the prison, simply looking for a place where she could see the moon. Or maybe Billy waited for her there. He'd take her in his arms, they'd sink in the grass, and then—what would happen next, I wasn't entirely sure. How did they remove their clothes? What if the grass held nettles and burrs? Did Billy carry a packet of Trojans in his jeans pocket, and if so, where did he get it? In a find-a-word I'd once spotted c-o-n-d-o-m on a right diagonal, but the word wasn't in the list and must have been an accident. Mornings I'd find Al flat on her bed, staring up at the ceiling. Against the pillow her fanned hair seemed to float, and I could see her at the very bottom of the quarry, her bones gone gray and sinking into the muck.

"Maybe," Mom said, "I should talk to Al about protection."

At that I looked up. Mom's head was tucked, her hands patting meatloaf into a pan. Her hair was Nice-and-Easy brown, curling around her ears, and later, years later, I'd figure out how impossibly young she was that summer—no more than thirty-two.

"Protection?" I asked.

Mom glanced at me, and her face pinked.

"Never mind," she said. "Go ask Al if she's eating tonight."

"You might ask her," I said. "About protection, I mean."

But I'd gotten into the habit of speaking too soft for anyone to hear. Mom stooped to slide the meatloaf into the oven, and when I went to the door and shouted at the shed, my voice came to me like a surprise.

Al didn't get pregnant, not that summer. Instead, Mom was the one who sat down at the breakfast table one morning after Dad left, looked into her just-filled coffee cup, and said in a slow voice, "I've thrown up three times this morning and coffee is the last thing I want." She set down the cup and gave it a push for punctuation. "We know what that means."

I didn't know what it meant, not at first, but in the days that foot-dragged into August, Mom's face was ash, and she'd return to bed the minute Dad's sedan disappeared from the drive. On her back she stared up at the ceiling, her face a stone.

Sometimes she spoke.

"Al cried all night," she said. "When she was a baby. Did I ever tell you? Loud enough to wake the neighborhood, hard enough to burst her own lungs. That's what I thought. I had no way to know if it was possible, for a baby to kill itself crying. Once I can remember I was standing with her at the top of the stairs, and I thought it would be so easy. I could say I tripped. It was an accident."

She shifted her head and looked at me. "I shouldn't be telling you these things," she said. "I shouldn't have thought them."

She looked back at the ceiling and went on. "And you—you hardly made a peep. Two years old and still you had nothing to say, and so I got you in my lap, you squirming and struggling, your face redder than a tomato but still not making a sound. I had to pry your mouth open. I thought maybe you didn't have a tongue, that somehow we'd forgotten to check."

She sighed. "There must be something wrong with me. I must be a terrible mother."

"Can I help?" I whispered, and she nodded, so I learned to make Tuna Helper, strip beds, and fold towels so Dad wouldn't come home, look about, and say, "Christ. The whole damn house has gone to pot." After supper I sat by him on the carpet and listened to Walter Cronkite, but all I could tell was something kept happening in distant places: Pakistan, Tibet, Northern Ireland. Mom stayed in the kitchen, rubbing at the clean counter with a sponge, so Dad explained to me the threat of leveraged buyouts, the outrage of overeducated and practically adolescent bosses who always wore suits, never left their desks, hadn't worked for the company for fifteen years as Dad had.

"Things are tough at the office," I told Al.

She glanced down at my find-a-word, an advanced edition with words like *Irrawaddy* running backwards and diagonally up and down the page.

"Why are you always doing those," she said. It wasn't a question.

"And Mom," I persisted. "I think she needs help."

Al leaned over, took up my pencil, and circled *perambulate* and *orienteering* in two quick loops. "There," she said. "All done."

I tried again, dropping my voice low. "I think there might be something wrong with her."

Al took a step back, crossed her arms, and looked hard at me. "Cassie," she said, "you need a hobby. A normal one like decoupage or modern dance."

Turning on her heel, heading for the patio, she added, "And quit spying on Billy and me."

Later, Mom came down the basement stairs while I fed towels into the washer. She was smiling bright, but her face looked pale as soap flakes.

"I suppose I can make over the sewing room," she said. "It's small, but there's a window at least, and with the right wallpaper, some cheery little ducks or rabbits, it'll be all right."

Mom still wore her bathrobe, the kind that zips up the front and has pockets on the sides to hold crumpled Kleenex. Her hair on one side was pillow-flat. I tried to picture happy rabbits and ducks, a mobile hanging above the crib that jingled *hush little baby don't say a word* when you wound it up. A boy, I thought, would make Dad grin. Someone to watch the evening news with, help him make the backyard weedless and green. Someone he could raise to be a smart success, far beyond the threats of transfer, buyout, layoff. As for Mom, she would hang up her robe, give herself a Lilt home perm, give Al and me one too, though Al would cry when it didn't turn out right, announce she wasn't going to show herself at school, not like this. Dad would come in from the office whistling and at the dinner table we'd tell him nothing of importance because there was nothing of importance to tell. The baby laughed today, we would report. The baby sat up. The baby is starting to crawl.

"Let's hope," Mom said, "your father keeps his job."

"He'll be home any minute," I replied.

She nodded. "I'm going up to shower," she said. "Don't put any sheets in with those towels. They get lint all over everything."

Then, from the top of the stairs she called, "Cassie? What are Billy and Al up to?"

"They're talking," I said, and it was as if we were all back to normal.

The night before Mom drove herself to Columbus—returning in the late afternoon, right before Dad got home, never speaking again of babies, bunnies, and ducks—the whistle sounded. It grew and spread, a flapping sheet, and I heard Dad's slippers shuffle past my door. Across the hall Al's bed was empty, and later, after Dad fell asleep, I would creep downstairs and unlock the sliding-glass door so she could get back in.

The whistle dropped. It faded like a dream, and that's

when I heard it: crying, muffled, as if into a pillow. I tiptoed down the hall and crawled into bed next to Mom. She was on her side, her face hidden from me, and she lay so still I thought maybe I'd only dreamed her sobs.

Then she whispered, "A D-and-C."

"What did you say?" I whispered back. I knew the word, of course, had learned it right along with *vasectomy* and *cloister.*

"A woman's thing," she said. "Your father won't even want to ask."

I imagined her voice carrying downstairs, out into the streets, mixing itself up with the siren, alarming the whole neighborhood or at least those who remained. I imagined Mrs. Reardon sitting straight up in bed or as straight up as her curved belly would allow. "Take me," she might shout, and up and down the street the plea would become a thin chorus: *Take me, take me, take me.*

"Do you think?" Mom whispered. "Should I?"

She shivered and I realized she'd started to cry again, silently, all sound smothered by the pillows. I touched my hand to her back, her shoulders, her hair. Against me she felt very small, just a curl of a being, the way I must have felt to Al. The whistle stopped. It dropped like a net.

How many are there? I used to ask Al.

Three this time, I think.

Three women in prison-blue smocks and baggy pants running hard and in bare feet. That's the story Al had told me, but in my mind I saw something else: a whole flood of women bursting through the reformatory gates, an ocean of blue that spilled onto Collins Avenue, then separated into rivers, creeks, and single, solitary streams. The whistle came again, rising, spreading, vibrating against the cage of my ribs years after they'd enclosed the prison in twelve-foot barbed wire, electrified. "'Sokay, 'sokay," I whispered to Mom. With my finger I wrote into her nightgown, into her skin i-r-r-a-w-a-d-d-y, o-r-i-e-n-t-e-e-r-i-n-g—the letters blending together into a simple caress, into a single voiceless *go*.

The Cheating Kind

"Here's a question," Marla said, slapping shut the *Cosmo* and pulling a Marlboro from the pack on the floor between us. It was a Wednesday, after school, and I was slumped down to my elbows on the thin carpet, staring at *General Hospital* on Marla's old black-and-white. The cold March sun shone through an uncurtained window, and the yelp of a dog drowned out the TV's sound. Until Marla spoke, I'd been scowling, lighting Marlboros end to end. I'd been wondering when something was going to happen— not on *General Hospital* but in our lives.

Marla lived on Prospect Street, where the lawns were shrunken and mangy dogs growled and struggled against their heavy chains. It was the part of town where things happened. Every Monday in the paper, I'd read all about the brawls and break-ins and, once, a murder just two houses down from Marla's. Never mind that the woman—who thrust a steak knife into her husband's chest when he went after her with his fists—was never jailed. On Prospect Street,

I expected to find life that was bursting, raunchy, and raw. On every corner I believed I'd see thieves, drunkards, and fortune tellers.

Marla looked a little like a fortune teller herself with her dangly earrings and her nails filed into witchy points. Or else she reminded me of a wicked and alluring picture of Eve I once saw in vacation Bible school. Instead of apples, she offered Marlboros and *Cosmopolitan* as the fruits of knowledge.

When Marla said she had a question for me, I sat up straight. I waited for her to read in *Cosmo* a quiz that asked how easily we could be seduced or if we were the cheating kind. Those quizzes would send a shivery thrill through me, and I always answered yes, I just might have it in me to be the cheating kind. But on this day, Marla didn't open the *Cosmo.* She puffed a chain of fat smoke rings, then turned to me and said, "If you could be anyone you wanted, anyone at all, who would you be?"

I looked down at my socks and listened to the yelping dog.

"Well?" Marla said.

It wasn't that I had no answer. I had too many. I wanted to be a princess and a pauper, a cherub and a thief. I wanted to be like Eloise Crofton, my former best friend, who had perfect posture and a father who owned a chain of H&R Blocks. I wanted to be like Marla, bleach my hair blonde, line my eyes in black pencil, and belong to Prospect Street with its dandelions, dogs, and murderous steak knives.

"I have no idea," I told her.

Marla eyed me, her lips pursed, her dark eyes narrowed. She'd peered at me the same way the first time I asked her for a cigarette, in the girls' bathroom at school. "Ellen Kirby," she said, "you do not have the aura of someone who smokes." Later, when she'd asked if she could borrow my copy of *The Scarlet Letter*, I pursed my lips, studied her, and replied, "Marla Rausch, you do not have the aura of someone who would read *The Scarlet Letter*."

Whenever Marla tried to read my aura, I held my face in a carefully arranged picture of innocence. I would cock my head to one side, make my eyes as wide and clear as windows. It was the same disguise I put on for my mother when I wanted her to believe I'd done nothing wrong and would never tell a lie. A strong, sudden wind must have knocked over the vase on the mantel. Father or the cleaning woman must have cut into the cake meant for company.

"Really," I told Marla now. "My mind's blank. You go first."

"All right," she said, settling back against the couch. "I'll tell you who I might want to be."

She sipped her Coke, then rested the bottle against her legs. Her legs were long and hot-waxed smooth, and though it was barely March, she wore cutoffs and a pink-striped tube top, trying to create the aura of summer.

She said, "I might want to be a courtesan."

I stared at her. "You want to be a hooker?"

"No, no. Not a hooker. A *cour-te-san.*" Her Ohio Valley twang smoothed out into lotion-soft sound. The word sounded strange, pleasingly sinful, and I shivered.

"I'll live in a grand salon," she went on. "With tapestries and mirrors and chandeliers everywhere. Kind of like your house, only it won't be in Ohio. It'll be someplace exotic like West Egg."

Marla had been reading my copy of *The Great Gatsby.* Though I'd already told her that in the end Gatsby gets shot and dies, she read fifty pages of it every night and would say to me every morning, "I can't wait to find out what happens."

"There's no such place as West Egg," I pointed out to her now, and I was about to say that my house, whose inside Marla would never see, had no tapestries or tacky mirrors and only one small chandelier in the front hall. But Marla had opened the *Cosmo* again. She paged to the back and pointed to an ad for satin sheets, midnight blue.

"I'm saving up for these."

"You're saving up for what?" called a voice from the kitchen.

The back door slammed, and in a moment, Marla's mother stood over us. She looked down at the satin sheets and snorted. "And how are you going to save up $59.95 if you don't get off your skinny ass and get a job?"

"Oh, Mom." Marla waved her hand as if her mother were some pesky insect.

Her mother walked back into the kitchen, her voice rising to carry through the thin walls. "The truth hurts, don't it, Marla?"

I stood up to follow.

"You never answered my question," Marla observed, then let me go. She was used to my tagging around after her mother when she came home from work. Her name was Bernice, but she told me to call her Bernie like her friends did, and on Marla's fourteenth birthday, she'd made us rum and Cokes with slices of lime. She neither laughed nor scolded when I got sick. Just stroked my head with gentle, work-rough hands as I hunched over the toilet.

Bernie did piecework at a fiberglass factory outside town, and weekdays at 4:15 she marched into the kitchen, slopped Clorox into a plastic bowl, and soaked her hands, speckled red with a fiberglass rash. When she reached up to grab the bowl, a gap appeared between her T-shirt and jeans, and I could see the pale, soft-looking flesh mottled with red bumps and streaks.

"So what'd I miss on *General Hospital* today?" Bernie usually asked—while other mothers in other kitchens asked about school, chores, and homework—and then we'd talk about the soaps or the tattooed foreman who kept pestering her to come out with him for a beer. Punctuating our conversation was the constant back-and-forth between Bernie and Marla:

"I thought I told you to take the chicken out of the freezer."

"I don't eat animal flesh, Mom. I told you. I'm just having a Coke for supper."

"You can't do one little thing for me, can you? How'd I get such a lazy-assed daughter, anyhow?"

"JEEE-sus Christ."

And then Marla would stomp into the kitchen, fling open the freezer, and slam the frozen-hard package of chicken parts on the counter.

I'd stand between them, my head turning from mother to daughter and back again. Their voices were loud, shrill, painful to the ears, and yet I didn't hear any real anger in their words. It was like the exercises I did in theater-arts class, a way to limber up vocal cords kept hushed too long.

But today there was no shouting. Bernie didn't ask me about my afternoon, and she didn't tell me about hers. She flew from the Clorox bowl into the bathroom and back again. She spun and whirled until I grew dizzy with watching, and all the while she cursed and muttered about showering, resetting her hair, and maybe borrowing Marla's blue velour blouse.

Marla stood in the doorway and watched for a long time. Finally she said, "You have a date, Mom?"

At home my mother set the table. She folded the cloth napkins and lay them parallel to our plates. I brought in the silverware from the kitchen, and as I followed her around the table, I told her I was going to Eloise Crofton's after supper.

"You just got home," she murmured.

"I had drama club today."

"You were out last night too."

"*Mother*—"

She glanced at me, and I quickly slipped into my innocent disguise.

"The other girls are going," I said, then smiled sweetly.

On my mother those three words—*the other girls*—worked like an *Open Sesame*. Nothing, she believed, was more important than fitting in.

"Homework?" she murmured, and I looked down at the forks and knives to hide my smile.

"We're doing it together at Eloise's."

"Well. You might invite Eloise over here sometime. We haven't seen her in months."

She had moved to the sideboard and was searching the drawers for matches to light the candles. She was always reading *Better Homes* and coming up with ideas like lighted candles and cloth napkins for what was only a weekday supper. For a second, I imagined reaching into my pocket and offering her my own, maybe lighting up a Marlboro right there and telling her I wasn't going to Eloise's tonight but to Marla's.

"You know Marla," I'd say. "Bernice Rausch's daughter?"

If I thought my mother would forbid me to go, shout after me as I stormed out of the house, I might have done this. I would have enjoyed a brief burst of drama, relished the role of the fugitive who's been caught and has to come out shooting. But none of this would happen. My mother didn't believe in loud voices and slamming doors. She would only look at me with mild perplexity, the way she did when I put on bright green eye shadow. She would say, "Well, if that's what you really want."

That's what she'd said to my father, three years before when he stayed out late most nights—working, he said. I watched one night from the upstairs landing as he came through the door and they stood murmuring in the front hall.

"Well, if that's what you really want," my mother had said quietly, firmly. And I thought I saw my father sag a bit, as if the air had suddenly left him. I waited—for raised voices and sharp tones and maybe the word *divorce.* But my father nodded once, stepped through the door, and they moved together into the living room. The next night he appeared at the dinner table, and when my mother asked him to pass the pepper, I wanted to cry out, "What is it? Something happened. I know it did." But I didn't. I knew they'd only look at me, heads cocked, eyes like Windexed windows.

"Did you hear a noise, honey?" my father might have asked.

"Probably the wind," my mother would have said.

So I stayed silent as my mother lit the candles, and later I sat up straight at the table and closed my eyes during the blessing. My mother, I decided, would never know about Marla. She would never, with a dubious look and a few quiet words, show me that I was on my way to becoming someone I didn't really want to be.

Bernie did have a date with a man named Bob, and though Marla had never met him, she said she could read his aura and it was bad.

"And just how do you know that, Miss Cosmic Perception?" Bernie had asked her that afternoon.

"Mom, you talk to the guy for two minutes, and he says, 'Let's spend a quiet evening alone.' I mean, Christ."

"So? He's a romantic."

"He's a lech. A sleaze. I don't even want to meet him."

But at seven o'clock, Marla and I were crouched at the windowsill. The neighbor's dog barked and growled, and my skin tingled as I waited to see a man who was a lech and a sleaze.

I didn't expect to see the Cadillac, its silver paint gleaming, or the pressed khaki pants and crew-neck sweater, a handsome man's face smiling shyly. He looked wholesome and athletic, like old pictures I'd seen of the Kennedys, though he reminded me of someone else too. His cheeks were shaded soft pink, and he hugged a small grocery sack to his chest.

"Bastard," Marla breathed.

No, I thought, blinking and looking again. *Bob Crofton.*

Bob Crofton who promised to save you money at tax-time. Bob Crofton, the father of the straight-standing Eloise.

He was as surprised to see me as I was him, and when Bernice introduced us, he gave a quick nod. I looked down at his hands, saw he wore no ring, and for a second, I pictured my own father walking through this door. I looked back up, and as I glared at Bob Crofton, his face turned from pink to red. I opened my mouth—to say I already knew who he was and his wife and daughter too—but then he gave me that shy, nervous smile. I shut my mouth, suddenly confused about who I was supposed to protect.

Bernie was telling us how she met Bob that afternoon at the Sohio station. I could see it: Bob in his Cadillac at the full-service island, watching as Bernie hopped out of her Pinto to pump her own gas. Maybe it was the damp curl clinging to the curve of her neck that drew him out or the way she deftly positioned the nozzle in the tank, then turned to the open hood to check the oil. Here was a woman who didn't need a man, he might have thought, or not for such trivialities as gassing up the car or paying bills. Here was a woman who didn't mind getting a little dirty. And I could see him leaping over the concrete divider, giving a cavalier bow, and taking hold of the dipstick, their fingertips touching for the first time.

"So where are you girls off to tonight?" Bernie asked. She took the sack from Bob and pulled out two six-packs of Black Label beer.

"Nowhere," Marla said sourly.

"It's a beautiful evening," Bob remarked.

Marla glowered at him. I toed the thin carpet with my sneaker.

"Maybe you could go over to Ellen's," Bernie said.

Bob jumped and turned his pink face to me. He did our taxes and with his wife had attended my mother's *Better Homes*–inspired summer solstice backyard brunch. For a moment, there was no sound. Even the dog was silent. Marla looked at me too, a flicker of expectation on her face. But I was more interested in Bob. He stared at me with eyes that were wide and pleading, and I felt a surge deep within me, a certainty of power that thrilled me more than any *Cosmo* quiz ever could.

"Ye-sss," I said slowly, as if I were actually considering Bernie's suggestion. "We could go visit with my parents." Bob's eyes widened even more. I wondered how much longer before he dropped to his knees before me.

"Or," I said after a very long pause, "we could take a drive. *If* we had a car."

In an instant, my fingers were closed over the keys to the Cadillac.

"We might get thirsty," I said.

And then, with one of those six-packs snug beneath my arm, I headed with Marla out the door. "Be careful!" Bernie shouted after us, and Bob called, "Take your time. But not too much time. Come back at ten, okay?"

I grinned at Marla, expecting her to be proud of me. Instead, she muttered all the way to the car, "Jesus Christ, Ellen. You don't have a license. What the hell do you think you're doing?"

"Don't worry," I told her. "My dad's let me drive the station wagon a hundred times. And I won't get caught. I never do."

And so it happened that from seven to ten every Wednesday night, the silver Cadillac was mine. The car leapt forward at a touch of my toe. The wheel felt slick and cool in my hands. I always drove fast, as if we were being pursued. I yowled at the swoop and drop of my stomach as we shot over hills and skidded around curves. The nights blended and blurred like the countryside flying by. Houses, barns, fields, cows. Melting snow, spring rain, hot red summer sunsets. In this car we were no longer fourteen, bored, talking about who we might want to be. We were beyond age, beyond limits, speeding faster than time itself.

Or at least I was. Marla never quite settled into the leather seat. She never accepted my offers to give her the wheel. She always wore a seatbelt. As spring turned to summer and the air grew thick and heavy, her fingers gripped the armrest and even her lips seemed to pale.

"Slow down!" she cried as we sped down a straight stretch of road. I pressed the gas pedal flat to the floor. The speedometer needle pushed past 75, past 80.

"Relax," I shouted back, motioning to the surrounding

soft blur of corn. "Who's going to catch us out here?"

"Ellen!"

I hit the brake and the Caddy skidded to a halt. I turned to her, scowling.

She said, "This isn't fun anymore. Why don't we go over to your house. We could watch TV."

"Oh, sure, Bob would love that." Not to mention my mother, I thought. I pictured her, face frozen, as she eyed Marla's bleached hair and black-lined eyes. "How do you do," she would say with lips that hardly moved.

"Listen," I said to Marla, shifting into gear again. "If you're not having fun, you can stay home."

At that, she shut up, and I recalled the night I'd shown up late and found Marla hunched against the couch. Her head was bowed over my copy of *Ethan Frome.* The instant she saw me, she jumped up, dropped the book, and said, "Let's go."

"Where's Bernie and Bob?" I had asked, and as Marla glanced up at the ceiling, then down at her toes, I'd felt the goose bumps spread across my arms.

"So," I said now, keeping the car at a steady fifty-five until Marla settled down. "Are we together on this?"

She nodded, reached down between her shoes, and pulled out a beer. I finished mine and tossed the empty into the backseat. Then I laughed as I imagined Bob Crofton turning into a lonely alley on his way home that night, glancing furtively about before depositing an armful of cans into a dumpster. Or I imagined him red-faced and shrugging when his daughter Eloise missed the Burberry raincoat I'd swiped from the backseat.

Marla shook her head, her lips pressed tight, when she saw me take the coat, but she didn't hiss *No, Ellen* the way she did when I tucked dimestore lipsticks into the waist of my jeans or wrote answers to World History quiz questions on the inside of my arm. She even smiled a little the night I paraded that stolen raincoat right past Bob, daring him with a wicked grin to try to take it back.

He said nothing, and the next week when he handed us the six-pack of Black Label beer, a ten-dollar bill was slipped between the cans.

"Take a look," I said to Marla, handing her the ten and slipping behind the wheel. "Just think how much we'll take him for the next time."

Marla slammed the door.

"What's your problem?" I said.

She held the ten tweezerlike between two fingers, and dropping it on the seat between us, she said, "I'm not some hooker."

I grabbed the bill and slapped it back into her lap, then jerked the car into reverse. We shot backwards, gravel spinning out from beneath the tires. As we headed down Prospect Street, a mangy old dog tried to chase us, but the chain caught and choked it back.

"Fucking stupid dog," I said and liked the sound of those words coming from my mouth.

Marla stared straight ahead, her face pale, not a trace of red in her lips. She looked bloodless, like Bernie did each night when we brought the car home: sitting at the kitchen table, smoking and scratching her speckled hands as Bob popped up and said, "Good, good, just in time. Keys?" Then slipped out the door.

But never mind Bernie and Bob, I told Marla as we flew over the back roads past blurs of corn and beans. Maybe for them this was sleaziness and dirt, but for us it was something else: drama and romance, maybe even the shining moment of our lives. Just fourteen years old, and we had Bob Crofton on a string. All we had to do was twist him this way and that and he'd shower us with gold. With cheap beer, cold cash, and a long, silver Cadillac filled with gas.

"You've got it mixed up," Marla said. "He's got *us* on a string."

"Not me," I said.

"No," Marla said quietly. "Not you."

Something in her voice, in the way she looked down at her hands folded in her lap, made me feel as if I were being accused, and without thinking, I snapped, "Settle back and enjoy it. Your mother certainly is."

At that, I shut my mouth and gripped the wheel tight in both hands. I hoped I hadn't really spoken. I hoped I'd only imagined saying such words. But when I glanced at Marla, she pressed back against the door as if I might strike her. She stared at me, not blinking even once.

"I didn't mean that," I said, and I cocked my head, trying to look guileless, sweet, and sorry. As if she believed me, Marla nodded and lit a Marlboro. At the next intersection I turned onto a pockmarked dirt road and pressed down on the gas.

"You were right about Bob," I went on. "He's a lech, a sleaze, just like you said."

The car bounced over rocks and ruts. Around us the sky was dull gray, tinged with yellow, like an old bruise. It was the kind of evening when a storm might strike at any moment, or maybe it wouldn't rain at all and the next day would dawn just as hot and still as this.

"We'll tell him to stop coming over," I said. "We'll threaten to tell his wife. Bernie knows he's married. Why does she still see him?"

Marla looked at me.

She said, "Why do I still see you?"

Her tone was light. We could almost have been poring over a *Cosmo* and considering how easily we could be seduced or if we were the cheating kind. But the words were edged, like sharp nails on the tips of gentle fingers. My foot lifted from the gas. I twisted toward her, my mind a jumble of impossible replies: "What do you *mean?*" and "Because we're *friends.*"

Before I could say a word, Marla's gaze shifted to the windshield. She sucked in her breath, and her eyes went wide. There was a jolt, then rapid sharp bumps. I looked ahead. Rushing at us was a solid wall of green.

It was only slender stalks of corn, ripe and ready for picking, that we hit. They gave way easily, and Marla, of course, didn't die.

It would be an easier story to tell if she had—the stuff of high drama like Gatsby face down and bleeding in a pool, the romance of a steak knife shivering between two ribs. I couldn't simply walk away then, pretend it had all never happened, brush off my acquaintance with Marla like a fine layer of dirt.

"We'll have to get a tow truck," Marla said, looking down at the Cadillac's front end shoved through rows of broken stalks, the tires dug into soft, rutted earth. She stepped carefully around the undamaged plants, shook her head, and said, "We'll need help."

A drop of blood clung to her lip, and she touched a finger to it. Probably I should have asked her, "Are you hurt?" But I was already thinking ahead to the tow truck, the sheriff, the call to my mother. I saw Bob Crofton shaking his head and saying no, of course he didn't give two fourteen-year-olds his Cadillac to drive.

"I'll go," I said. I took one step back. Crisp leaves and stalks crackled beneath my feet. I kicked into the road a crushed, empty can of Black Label. "You stay here. I'll get help."

I took another step back, then paused for the jagged bolt of lightning to strike me dead or for Marla to read my aura and explode, "Oh, like hell I'm going to let you leave me here." But the sky stayed the same bruised rainless gray, and Marla remained by the car and nodded as if she believed me, as if she trusted me to do this one small, honest thing.

"You stay here," I said again, turning now to run.

Tender Foot

"I'm coming to realize," Mike says, "that we'll never be friends."

You're sitting at the small table in Mike's kitchenette, finishing off a bottle of red wine. A celebratory bottle, you had thought, since tonight's the first time Mike has invited you over for longer than a minute while his son visits.

"I want you and Daniel to get to know each other," he'd said when you called. "I want you to be friends."

Your last boyfriend, Stephen, had two children who came to stay on alternate weekends plus holidays, so you already know how to play Don't Spill the Beans. You know the names of all the plastic dinosaurs Mike's five-year-old son spreads across the living-room floor. You know to sit cross-legged and quiet until Daniel chooses to play with you.

Now Daniel lies on the floor in front of the TV, a thin blanket pulled to his chin. He stares, eyes unblinking, at the screen. You open the window an inch so the smoke from your cigarette drifts out. Mike keeps his voice hushed. He's talking about his ex-wife.

"It hit me this morning when I went to pick up Daniel. She didn't even ask if I wanted to come in. We can't even be *polite* to each other."

He rubs his eyes as if he's weary, reaches to refill his glass. In the light of the bare bulb that hangs over the table, his skin looks sallow. For the first time you notice how it sags, heavy, along his jawline. "What's a decade or two between friends?" That's what you usually say. "I can hardly keep up with you as it is." Sometimes you say that too. But tonight there is a table space between you, and Mike looks almost old. His eyes, usually dark and shining like polished stones, open wide even when you're making love, are bloodshot with heavy lids half closed. You tell yourself that after this cigarette you'll get your coat. After this glass of wine, you'll go home. From the window at your back comes a finger of cold air. You shiver, then scoot your chair in before Mike sees.

"I'm sorry," he says. "You don't want to hear about Christine."

"No, no, it's okay. You and I are friends, right? We can talk."

You stamp out your cigarette, then check an impulse to carry the ashtray, overflowing, to the wastebasket. Too domestic. Too presumptuous. You avoid any move suggesting you think of yourself as more than a friend. When a door is closed in Mike's apartment, you leave it that way. If the telephone rings when he's in the shower, you let the machine pick it up. Once, when Mike went out for beer, a woman named Angela called.

"It was great seeing you," she said.

She said, "Call me."

"A friend," Mike explained when he played the message back. You studied your fingernails and shrugged like you hadn't been paying attention. In a way, you hadn't. To keep from thinking of a woman named Angela, you recalled a game you used to play with your brothers. Tender Foot, they called it, and the rules were simple: Through the woods beyond your house you were to walk barefoot, your initiation into becoming a toughened Indian scout. If you snapped a stick or sneezed just once, you died, that's all. You think of that game now—the knife-sharp pebbles and twigs that sounded like gunshots, the thick calluses you spent your teens pumicing smooth. The woods had not really been woods at all but a thin stand of ragged trees. The trees edged a spreading subdivision that, despite being three states and a day's long drive away, looks identical to where you live now. You empty the wine bottle into your glass. To Mike you say, "Go on. I'm listening."

As he talks, you lean forward in your chair. You squeeze your knees together, press your nails into the fleshy part of your palm. You try to look open to hearing what you don't want to hear at all.

at me like I was no one," he says. "Not her
~~~en~~ years. Not the father of her son, the man
~~over~~. She looked at me like I was just a body
stan~~~ ~~~ er front porch."

You shake your head, cluck your tongue, decide that
another cigarette will be all right. You can turn your chair to
the window then. You can shift your gaze away from Mike's
slow-moving lips, his hands folding and unfolding a paper
napkin, again and again, until the creases wear thin.

"She didn't even ask me in," Mike says.

You nod as if to say, "I understand." Across the room
Daniel squirms and makes a little whine. Mike snaps his
gaze to him. Daniel frowns. He tugs too hard at the blanket's
frayed hem, uncovers his bare toes.

"Daddy," he says, and Mike starts to rise.

"No," Daniel cries, "I don't want you." Mike sits down.

"Daddy!" Daniel insists, then "No, go away." Mike stands,
sits, stands, sits and Daniel giggles, delighted with what has
turned into a game.

Through all of this, you hold your breath, like you did
when you were ten years old and laid out like a corpse in the
woods. Each time you died, your brothers added to how
long you had to lie still—ten minutes, fifteen, twenty, twen-
ty-five—and then they would shout, "Okay, new game,
you're alive." Through the long minutes you never twitched,
not even when they tickled your chin with milkweed puff or
buried you in slick moist leaves. You were better at playing

dead than anyone. Or so you thought until a year later when you watched the lifeguards pull a girl from the deep end of the town pool. Her belly was ballooned as if she were pregnant. Her eyes were flat like nickels. Your girlfriends paled, covered their eyes. They pivoted away on delicate bare heels. With your brothers you watched, fascinated, awed, as the lifeguards did their work, mechanically and without hope. The girl's skin was gray-white and all bumpy like schoolroom paste, and though you later learned she was only eight, she looked ancient to you, as if for her whole decades had passed at the bottom of the pool.

"Dad-dy, Dad-dy." Daniel's voice has dropped to a singsong drone. Mike turns back to the table. His eyes flicker as if he's startled, then pleased, to find you sitting here. The corners of his mouth turn up. For the first time tonight he takes your hand. The suddenness of his touch nearly takes your breath.

"Thanks for coming," Mike says. "I mean it. I'm glad you called. I'm glad we can talk."

Yes, glad, a good thing. This is what you think. As his hand moves over yours, you feel a surge of something, radiating out to your fingertips, spreading through your thighs, making your body start to hum. It reminds you of the night you sat drinking wine and listening to Ella Fitzgerald. Just like this, Mike took your hand, lifted you up. As Ella sang "Cheek to Cheek," he swung you around the living room, spun you out, pulled you in, until your heart pumped strong and Ella's voice, so full, so rich, prodded something deep inside, making it grow, making it bloom.

Beneath the table your thighs rub themselves slowly, pleasurably together. On the tabletop, you keep your hand folded in Mike's for a minute, maybe two, until you see a muscle in his forearm give a jump. You slip your fingers free. It's the same whenever you make love. Afterward, you lie against him. You watch his chest rise and fall, imagine how his fingers look as they drift up and down your spine—until you hear him sigh or feel him shift his weight. That's when you get up, get dressed, smoke a cigarette, tell him you have to go. You've learned when to leave so he'll look wistful rather than relieved.

Christine, Mike says, looked so drawn this morning, as if she hadn't slept, as if she isn't well. He's taken up the paper napkin again. Christine, Mike says, won't even talk to him. When he telephones, she speaks in single syllables: yes, no, what, bye. "Oh," you reply. "I see." Across the room Daniel's eyelashes flutter, and you imagine how it will be later on: Mike gathering his son in his arms, the two slowly circling the room, turning out the lights, making sure the door is shut tight and locked. "Do you need to go to the bathroom?" Mike will whisper to his son. "Do you want the night-light on?" You light your cigarette, twist to the window, its shot of cold air. Outside there's a skinny, leafless tree and a vacant parking lot. The blacktop looks slick beneath streetlights.

Once, years before in another kitchen, you sat across

from a man named Gerald. As he talked about the woman he used to live with, you shook your head, clucked your tongue, tried not to look like you were falling in love. You were nineteen then or twenty, and just learning how to make yourself disappear. You were just learning that if you stayed too long, said too much, his face would go still and shadowed, like water beneath a glaze of ice. At such a moment you would grin at him and say, "The nice thing about you is I'm not at all in love with you." You made Gerald laugh, slap the tabletop, so the wine bottle jumped. For minutes after he'd chuckled to himself, said, "You're different, you know that? You're rare."

Ray had laughed, called you different too, and Dennis after that, then Tom, then Stephen. You think about them, how many of them there are. "He was a friend," you tell Mike whenever you let a name slip, Mike's lips curling as he spits back, "A *friend?* You mean, like we're *friends?*" No, no, not at all. That's what you say. But now you imagine them from Gerald to Mike, lined up shoulder to shoulder, all exactly the same with their scabby wounds and their toughened, tucked-away hearts. You think of the women too, women you've never met but have heard so much about, you know them almost intimately. Marjorie, Julie, Susan, Marlene. The ex-wives, ex-girlfriends, the ones they talk about, tell stories about, even weep about.

Christine you have seen, once, at the IGA on a Saturday afternoon. She stood with Daniel at the dairy case, was tall and slender with brown hair smoothed in a coil, her eyes unexpectedly an iridescent blue. Regal. That's the word that ran through your mind. Even in blue jeans and a flannel shirt, she could draw a second glance and another after that, could make you swear you'd seen her in a magazine or on TV—a movie star, a queen.

"The thing is," Mike says, "I can't stop thinking about her. Even after she looks right through me when I'm standing on her front porch."

You draw on your cigarette, its smoke like pepper inside your throat. Telling yourself this really is the last one, you murmur, "I know" and "Of course not." You mean it too. Of course he still thinks of her, all the time, this woman who was his wife, the mother of his son, who can appear so cool and distant, even in an IGA on a Saturday afternoon. Sometimes, at the bathroom mirror, you pull your hair back just like Christine's. It makes your eyes jump out, huge and hungry-looking in a face too narrow, too pale. You pull yourself up straight, tell yourself you must remember to smile more often than you do. You tell yourself that perhaps you made up Christine. She could well be chinless, short-waisted, with hair pulled back because it's unwashed. Maybe you only imagined she lifted the milk carton with a dancer's grace. After all, the instant you saw her, you turned away, left behind your grocery cart, though she didn't see you and wouldn't know who you were if she did.

"I can't stop thinking about her," Mike says again. He

clenches the napkin in his fist. The veins pop out on the back of his hand. You want to reach out and press each gently into place. You're about to do this—yes, why not? Christine isn't here and you are and this must mean something. Then Mike looks straight at you, and what he says next stops you dead.

"The thing is, I'm still in love with her."

You've known, of course, that this was coming. You've even rehearsed this moment in your mind. In your mind you've made Mike say, "I'm still in love with her," and in your mind you've nodded and murmured and touched his hand, lightly, imperceptibly. You've practiced. But it doesn't make a bit of difference. The breath still leaves, the next won't come. The air turns to liquid. It washes over the room in cold blue waves, and you can almost believe that if you checked, you'd find a deep stillness where a pulse should be. You remember the quiet woods, the leaves so soft beneath your back, your brothers watching as your body sank, sank, sank into the earth.

But all of this is only for a moment. Your brothers shout, "Okay, you're alive, new game!" Your pulse picks up its familiar rhythm once more. You kill the cigarette, shut the window, press your palms to the sill. It's like ice now.

There was a time when such a conversation could make you feel almost proud. Your nods and murmurs, you believed, confirmed you as grown-up, mature; you were handling it so well. You would twirl the stem of your wine glass, now and then making offhand remarks you hoped sounded sophisticated and adult: "Oh, love is out of the question," or "I'm glad you and I are only friends. That kind of thing will never happen to us." Now you can't think of anything to say, not even "I know" or "Yes, I understand." You feel the cold beneath your palms. You feel the warm vapor of your breath as it melts on the windowpane. You feel suddenly very tired, as if tonight you've grown old too, your joints arthritic stiff, your bones as dry and easily snapped as twigs.

"I'm sorry," Mike says. "You don't want to hear about Christine."

Before you can say, "No, no, it's all right," there's a rustling sound. Daniel has rolled out from his blanket. He lies curled up tight, shivering on the wood floor. In an instant Mike is out of his chair, across the room. He scoops Daniel up in his arms, says, "Hey there. How do you feel about bed?"

"Noooo," Daniel says, his protest half whisper and half hushed sob. "Just a hug," he says.

"Sure," Mike tells him. "Anything."

He presses his cheek to Daniel's. He hums a song he makes up just for them. Together their eyes close, their breathing in easy tandem. This is when you feel it: not an ache, not a pang, not any kind of emotion like jealousy or longing or love. What you feel instead is more like wonder— wonder that this time you've really done it, you've made your own heart stop. You could say to Mike, "I'm not at all in love with you," and it would be true. You could say, "That kind of thing will never happen to us," and this would be true too. Watching him cradle and sing to his son, you try to recall that night you danced in this room, your bare feet slipping over smooth floorboards, your fingers hot, damp, entwined. You try, but the memory has turned hazy and vague, like a story you once heard about somebody else.

"Listen," you say, standing, shaking out the numbness in your knee.

Mike glances your way.

"I have to go."

He nods, then holds a finger to his lips. Against him Daniel has gone limp, eyes closed, fingers still loosely pulling at the neck of his father's shirt. With an elbow Mike indicates your coat on the couch. His lips move but make no sound. *Drive carefully,* you think he means. *I will,* you mouth back though this night you came on foot.

Dog

What gets me about puppies is they're so small. Small and weak. Anything could happen to them. I'm running across the yard and don't see the little lump of fur before me. Until I hear the yelp and I jump up, while the very worst that could happen flashes like a blown bulb in my brain. Just a paw, nothing broken; it's okay. But it could have been a belly, a back. It could happen. My fault. It could.

That's what I thought when on my eleventh birthday, my parents took me to a pet store and told me to pick out a puppy. No. No way. I wasn't taking any chances on those toothpick-boned pups. Sure, they looked healthy and strong with shiny coats and pink wet tongues. But one look at their eyes told me stay away. Through the Plexiglas those eyes stared at me, into me, with so much trust, so much need for protection. Once home, this dog would be my responsibility. If anything happened, I'd be to blame. Even if I was miles away, it would be my fault.

At first my father couldn't believe it. He grinned. He dug an elbow into my mother's side.

"What a joker," he said.

"I think he means it," Mom replied.

"What are you talking about? It's man's best friend. Of course he wants a dog."

"No," I answered. "Thank you. No."

He tried turning stern. "Okay, funny guy. Enough is enough. We haven't got all day."

He tried making light. "If you're having trouble choosing, do eeny-meany-miney-moe." He added, "You know, once we wrap up here, we can visit the food court."

I shook my head, stood statue still. I imagined myself invisible, the way my brother Wayne and I used to do. That's what I'd done some weeks before when Dad had wanted to sign up for the YMCA's father-son softball league, even though just a slow stroll to first base would leave him gasping. "I don't think softball is quite the thing for Max," Mom had put in, and then Dad had urged me to try out for soccer or else take up a musical instrument, join the marching band.

"Just think of it," he'd chorused. "You could have the whole town whistling a happy tune. Our very own Music Man!"

"He's only trying to help," my mother had whispered to me. In the pet store, she whispered it again. Then she glanced toward the storefront and said, "Maybe Max would like a kitten." A kitten? Christ. They're even smaller than puppies. You might find it one morning just off the curb, eyes gluey with flies.

"No," I said. "No, thank you."

In the end, with my mother's mediation, I agreed to a goldfish. There was a pet I could deal with. They circle their own small world, and when they die, you flush them down the toilet. That's all. No one feels bad about it. No one thinks twice. For the single fish, Dad selected a tank that could have held several piranhas and a small sea turtle. He added a pink plastic bridge and a pair of deep-sea divers. He told me that when he was a boy, Jules Verne was his favorite author, that he'd have become a diver himself if he could only hold his breath. Really, if you thought about it, he added, his asthma was a lucky break for Mom, the only reason he'd been sitting behind that desk at Bank Ohio all those years ago when she walked in to inquire about passbook savings. Mom placed a soft hand on the back of my neck. I understood. He was trying, the best he could. How could we fault him for that?

That was in August. In December, for Christmas, my parents gave me a puppy. I came downstairs Christmas morning and there it was beneath the blinking tree, a big red bow at its throat. Other presents, a mountain of them, far more than we'd ever received before, reached past the windowsill, and I imagined that if you stacked them, one on top of the other, they'd reach to the roof, climb to the sky. But this thing, this puppy, I knew, was the big gift. Every year we got one. The year before, Wayne got his first bike. It was small with training wheels and a little bell that he loved to make ching-ching until I told him bells were for wusses. He pestered me to teach him to ride. "Bug off," I told him. "Drop dead." Lydia, one of the neighborhood girls, taught him how. She held him steady until he got the knack. She encouraged him to ring the bell.

The puppy was fat, squat, and spotted. It gnawed at the enormous ribbon around its neck. It waddled toward me, leaving behind on the carpet a small dark stain. I looked up at Mom and Dad. Mom started to smile, then gave up. Traitor, I thought. Hypocrite. Dad beamed. I looked down at the puppy. It was biting my bare toes.

"Looks like you have a new pal," Dad said.

I weighed my options. I could say, "No. No, I don't," or I could sidestep it, pretend I didn't see it, head straight to the mantle for my stocking. The night before, Mom had dragged out the box of mismatched mittens and old knitted caps. She'd pulled from it two stockings, mine and Wayne's. On her knees, she'd held both to the mantle, then glanced at my father in the chair beside her. Though he said nothing, did not seem to move or breathe, she must have seen something because she'd dropped Wayne's stocking back in the box and cheerily agreed when my father suggested we go to the piano and sing "Jingle Bells."

"Go on," Dad urged me. "Say hello to the little guy."

Mom gave a nod, and I knew what she would say to me if she could. I dropped to the floor. I clapped my hands. The puppy scampered toward me, tail-end squirming like mad. I saw Dad's arm creep around my mother's waist, watched her relax against him. For the first time in months she didn't look as if her body were strung with wires, taut and vibrating at the slightest disturbance in the air. She smiled at me and this time the smile stayed. We were trying, all of us, the best we could, the only way we knew how. Later, when Dad pulled out the Polaroid, I made noisy shows of delight.

"I knew a puppy was just the thing," Dad said. He told us stories of his boyhood dog that had to be given away when allergies set in.

"I think he looks just like the one I had," he said. "I wish I had a picture. I'm sure that's why he caught my eye."

He started to sneeze, and Mom told me to take the dog into the kitchen.

"No, no," my father gasped. He pulled out his handkerchief. His eyes looked watery, lids painfully puffed. The sneezes turned to coughs, terrible coughs like ripped burlap. I set my eyes on the puppy, no bigger than a stuffed sock. I could imagine in the backyard an owl swooping down from the sky, snatching it in its beak. I couldn't tell whether I wanted this to happen or not.

"It's the Christmas tree that's getting me," Dad managed to say a while later. To prove his point, he took the puppy in his lap, lifted it to his nose, took in what counted for him as a deep breath.

"All that musty pine," he said. "It's a wonder any of us can breathe."

The next morning my father and I sat at the kitchen table, the weak winter sun trickling in and making him look yellow. He'd slept sitting up in a living-room chair. This morning his eyes were raccoon-ringed and sunken deep, but his breath came without a scrape. My mother set a bowl of cereal in front of me and paused at the window. Her back was to us both.

"Glorious morning," Dad said. "This day is just plain glorious." He spread his arms wide as if he might burst into song.

"Well?" he said to me. "Don't you think?"

I nodded. It seemed the easiest thing to do.

"Mother?" he asked. "Don't you think so too?"

"Yes," she replied, still not turning from the window. "Glorious."

Drawing the bathrobe about her, she padded out to pick up the morning paper. I listened carefully for her slippered steps, waited for the sound of their return. I worried that one morning she would go out and not come back, a pale thin woman vanishing into pale thin air.

"So tell me," Dad said. "Have you come up with a name?"

"No," I said. The dog chewed at my sneaker, and I looked

down at it. I imagined digging my toe into its ribs, punting it like a football.

"Why not?" he asked. "Can't think of anything?"

I shrugged.

"Champ," he said. "That was my dog's name. I wouldn't mind another Champ."

I ate my cereal and didn't reply.

"Okay, you want to come up with your own name. Sure. Understood. What do you say to him when you want him to come here?"

"I say, 'Come here, dog.'"

"Well, name him Dog then. Plain, simple, a name you won't forget, eh?" Dad settled back and looked pleased.

So it became Dog. That's what my parents called it. That's what they told everyone who stopped by to call it.

"Kids," my father chuckled. "Go figure, huh?"

Through the front door streamed aunts and uncles, neighbors and friends, the couples who belonged to my parents' bridge club. Every one of them made Os with their mouths when they spotted Dog. "Would you look at that!" they exclaimed. "What a surprise." Then they'd glance at my parents. I could picture my mother saying over a game of bridge, "It's been hard on Max. He hasn't been—," my father quickly stepping in, "We're sure a puppy will do the trick."

"I'm going out to play," I would announce each time a new guest arrived.

"Don't forget Dog," Dad always said.

"Stay in the yard," Mom would add. She'd reach out, grip my shoulder, as if she wasn't really going to let me go. "Stay where I can see you."

The sun had disappeared, and the sky hung low and gray. In the backyards the neighborhood kids huddled together, fat as plums in snowsuits, their Christmas sleds useless by their sides. When they spotted Dog, they came running. Around it they formed a tight ring, crouching down and reaching mittens out to pet it. I hung back, plucked up the rope of a stray sled and slid it back and forth over the stiff brown grass. I imagined it would snow and I would be at the top of Old Man Hill in Legion Park, well out of my parents' sight. I would careen down the slick slope. I would expertly guide the sled around each sharp curve. I would miss the great oaks by the barest breath. Hard pellets of ice would sting my skin, pepper my eyes, and at the hill's bottom, I'd roll off and lie on my back. I'd stare up at the branches spread like fans against the sky.

This is what I imagined until I heard a bark, disappointed cries. Turning, I saw Dog dashing toward me. The sight of it made my fists ball, my head go dizzy light.

"Stupid shit!" I shouted. "I told you to stay!" Dog shrank back, whimpered, then sidled up to me again. It didn't listen. It would never learn. I lifted my boot. I was only going to give it a nudge, but Lydia, the girl who'd taught Wayne to ride his new bike, snatched the puppy away. The neighborhood kids stared until I wanted to protest, "Listen. You don't understand." Instead, I made myself stand oak-tree still. I sucked in deep breaths of air solid enough to plant me to the ground. I pointed a finger at Dog, ordered, "Stay," and started across the yard. Behind me Dog whined. I stepped carefully, knowing that at any moment it would dodge into my path. "But why can't I come too?" That's what Wayne used to cry. He'd run to keep up with me, my outgrown pants sliding around his skinny hips. "I'm here," he'd shout when I made believe that he was not.

"Ma-ax!" Wayne would wail. "I'm here, I'm here! Don't you see me? I'm here!"

Half a dozen kids his age, and he still had to tag after me everywhere I went, sneaking around behind me even after I'd smack him for it. Once he showed up when a bunch of us were sledding at Old Man Hill and when I told him to get lost, he proudly produced a first-aid kit—a scattering of Band-Aids, a tube of antiseptic cream, the useless stethoscope from his play doctor kit, just in case someone got hurt. You're such a wuss, I said. Why don't you just drop dead?

Out in back of the new houses, across the empty lots where they were planning to build more, into the woods of Legion Park and beyond Old Man Hill, there was an abandoned railroad track where I'd sometimes go and Wayne would sometimes follow. At one point it crossed a deep ravine, and through the wide gaps in the rotted boards, you could see the broken beer bottles below.

That's how Wayne died. He fell from that bridge while I

was at summer camp. Thirty-six feet, it said in the paper.

"I have two sons," my father used to boast. "We tried for a girl, but I guess I just didn't have it in me." Now when asked, he'd falter. "I have . . . a son. One son. Max. Yes, here he is."

Each night when we sat down at the supper table, Dad said the blessing. He mumbled something at the end about taking care of "our loved ones above." We never said Wayne's name. It was as if God Himself had issued a decree against it, as if the name might bring a biblical swarm of locusts. Once during the nightly blessing I peeked and saw Mom glancing up and around us. I thought she was looking to see if Wayne's ghost might be hovering there. When she spotted me spying, she shut her eyes.

"Where's Dog?" Dad asked as I passed him the peas. When I shrugged, he regarded me sternly. "Have you been remembering to brush him? When did you last take him out? Have you been watching to see there're no accidents?"

At that last question, I thought I saw my mother wince.

"Maybe I'm not old enough to look after a dog," I replied.

"Nonsense," Dad said.

Beside the bunk beds in my room he had placed a small cushioned basket for Dog. It yelped in its sleep. It whined and twitched and cried until I poked it, tossed a sneaker at it, and finally, flicked on the tank's blue light. The single goldfish shimmered and flashed. It suffered no nightmares, made no sound, and about its well-being no one ever asked.

My father never chuckled, "Fish. There's a name. Why don't you call it Fish?"

Maybe it had cancer, or rabies. That's what I told myself when, the day before New Year's, Dad and I took Dog to the vet. Maybe it had something horrible, deadly, a disease the pet store had kept hidden. The vet would shake his head, say in a low, grave voice, "I'm sorry, but we'll have to put him to sleep." Put it to sleep. Not kill it. Just make it close its eyes and lie still, a permanent nap. No one would blame us. My parents' bridge club friends would look sad and knowing and say such things happen, they're unavoidable. Dad would squeeze my shoulder, suggest one more time that I should join the marching band, and it would not be so bad, me in my uniform, lost in the group, blissfully brain-dead from the great blast of a tuba in my ear. A good boy, my father could say. A busy boy. He joined the marching band.

Instead, the vet gave Dog a shot, poked it some, and remarked that this was one healthy pup.

"Are you sure?" I asked.

They looked at me, my father and the vet.

"Relax," the vet told me. "You may just have the healthiest dog in the state of Ohio."

"Thank you," my father said. Then he choked, sneezed, and in between managed to add he wished he could say the same about himself.

In the waiting room Dog dashed forward on its leash, back between my legs, around one ankle, until we were all in a tangle. A woman sat on the couch, a dachshund cradled in her lap. She smiled at me.

"I hope he's all right," she said.

"Fine, fine," said my father. "He's as fit as a fiddle."

The words left my mouth before I could stop them: "You want him?" Her smile vanished, then came back, twisted and perplexed. I could feel my father's gaze hanging heavy over me, his breath like the rustle of dry paper.

"Joke," I added.

"Ha-ha," the woman replied, even though it wasn't funny.

A paper route, Dad said on the drive home. That would be the ticket.

"I had a paper route when I was younger than you," he said. "It was good for me, getting up every day at five, hitting the pavement by five-fifteen, early to bed and early to rise, Champ coming along for company. I would have kept it up if it hadn't been for this darned asthma. But you don't have such problems. No reason why you shouldn't have your own paper route."

On and on he went, his voice a hammer, each word a nail, securing fast and everlasting that picture of me as a god-damn paperboy, pedaling down the street in the predawn light, my moronically named dog yapping at my wheels, at risk of catching its neck in the spokes. Dog crouched on the floor, held fast by my ankles. I could feel its sides tremble each time my father shifted gears, hit the brake. I looked out the window. It had started to snow.

By noon, snow covered the ground. Drifts rose to the windows, and still it snowed, flakes heavy and wet. My father, after insisting he could shovel the walk and after giving the job a brave twenty-minute try, had spent the afternoon in bed. Mom rubbed his chest with Vicks. She made pots of hot lemony tea and telephoned Dad's office. Now Bank Ohio was called Bank US, with a new branch in the parking lot of the shopping mall. Dad was still the manager, and though it was no longer expected, he still went to work in jacket and tie. But under him these days were a bunch of what he called smart-alecky kids, just out of college and on their way to someplace else. No, no, nothing serious, Mom said into the phone to one of these kids. Yes, he'd be glad to hear that all was running smoothly, and yes, Happy New Year's to everyone there too. She left another message with the doctor's answering service, then returned to her trips up the stairs and down, tight-lipped and very quiet, as if this wasn't just another asthma attack. Twice I had asked her if I could take my sled out to Legion Park. Twice she had looked out the window and set her mouth into the straight line that said no, you may not. "I want you to stay in the yard," she said. "Stay where I can see you." She shivered, and I remembered how she used to ask, whenever Wayne or I got a sudden chill, "Goose cross your grave?"

Mid-afternoon the doctor's office phoned. I heard Mom murmur about the worst having passed and an appointment in the coming week. When she hung up, she paused for the first time that afternoon. She rubbed her temples as if trying to recall the one task she'd left undone. Then she crossed the room and stood over me. I was stretched flat in front of the TV, head half propped by a pillow so I could drift between old episodes of *Batman* and sleep.

"There's something I need to tell you," Mom said. She reached down to touch my hair. Cold dread, or maybe a draft from under the couch, crept up from my toes. "There's something I need to tell you" is how Mom had started things off the day she and Dad turned up, out of the blue, at my summer camp. Dad had been momentarily without words. Mom started to lower herself to the carpet beside me. Overhead the floorboards creaked. It was my father up, out of bed, about to catch his death. Mom snapped up, then shot up the stairs. She didn't return until it was time to get supper.

"Max," I heard her call from the kitchen. "Max, can you come here?"

I tucked myself into the tight space between the couch and picture window. Dog tried to squeeze in beside me. I gave its nose a finger-flick. It yelped, retreated, then stood there, eyeing me hopefully.

"Max," Mom called again. "I need to talk to you."

I could hear her moving through the house, opening

closet doors, pulling back drapes to check the snowy yard. At her heels I spied Dog, following along, nipping at her shoes. When she leaned over the couch and parted the drapes of the picture window, I didn't breathe. It wasn't until I heard an edge of panic in her voice that I popped up.

"Surprise," I said.

She jumped back, hands reaching for her mouth. Then she steadied herself, shook her head. Her chest fell, as if she'd been holding her breath too.

"Go wash your hands," she sighed. "It's almost time to eat."

When we sat down for supper that night, New Year's Eve, Dad was in his bathrobe and breathing easier. He murmured the blessing. He forgot to mention our loved ones.

"Max," he said. "How would you like a brother?"

It's hard for me, even now, to describe what I felt next. It's like trying to describe how it felt to clutch my sled and go belly down over the top of Old Man Hill. Rushing joy and bowel-loosening fear and an anger so deep, so primal, I can't believe, looking back, that such an emotion can be assigned to an eleven-year-old boy. First came the flash of believing, somehow, miraculously, Wayne was back, maybe hiding in the kitchen and waiting to pop through the swinging door. *Surprise!* It wasn't his body broken beneath that bridge, after all, but that of some other unlucky boy. Then I heard my mother say, softly, "Or a sister." Dad beamed, head bobbing, hands clasping together, as if this were Christmas morning all over again and here was the big gift, the one at which I should cry, "Oh! Oh, thank you!" I looked at my mother. She looked at her plate. Traitor. How could she? I knew then how it would be: a dog, a paper route, a new baby brother. "I have two sons," my father could say once more because, of course, she would bear him a son. And maybe once a year we would visit the cemetery by Legion Park and maybe my father would mumble something about our loved ones above. Or maybe he would not, and Wayne would drop from our lives just as surely as he'd dropped from that bridge.

By my chair Dog started to whine. I pushed back and said I needed to take it out.

"Don't leave the yard," Mom called after me as I pulled on my coat, headed for the door, Dog leashless beside me. She reached out her hand as if to grasp my shoulder, though I was already beyond her. "Stay where I can see you."

The snow had slowed to a few stray flakes, and the house roofs stood sharp against the blue-black sky. I found my sled in the garage. Dragging it along, I trudged across the street. Dog floundered through a drift somewhere behind me, panting hard. The most satisfying thing I could imagine at that moment was a car suddenly speeding down the street, missing me by inches, catching Dog in its wheels. It came out of nowhere, I would explain. Damn teenagers, my father would scowl. Of course this didn't happen, and we moved over yards, past the vacant lots, through the iron gates of Legion Park, and up to the top of Old Man Hill, where I plopped belly down on the sled and pushed off. I sped down the steep slope faster than I'd ever dared, not pulling back on the brake even once. Trees popped up in my path, inches before me, their rough bark scraping my coat sleeve and bruising my elbow as I flew by. For a wild moment I imagined aiming myself straight into one, making sure my father could never say, "I have two sons," but I was a coward and at the last second, I steered hard, whistled past, until finally I reached bottom, jumped up, grabbed my sled, and hurried home where I told my parents that I didn't know why but Dog had taken off.

Tonight my mother calls and says my father's emphysema has worsened and they're thinking of selling the house, moving someplace warm and dry like Arizona or New Mexico. Bank US is now Bank Global, with a sleek office tower rising up in Beijing and customer service representatives in Kildare. It seems, Mom explains, like the right time for Dad to retire, even if it is sooner than what they'd saved for. They'll all go—Mom, Dad, Robby, and even Dog, his back legs stiffened with arthritis and his breathing as labored as my dad's.

"Just picture it, Max," Dad gets on the phone long enough to wheeze. "Cactus, coyotes. We'll be home on the range."

"We'll buy a little house near a good doctor, a hospital," Mom says. "Maybe I'll find myself a part-time job." She sounds weary, as if she has not slept in years.

"I'll miss you," I tell them, and "Yes, of course. Not Thanksgiving but Christmas for sure."

What I really feel is relief, something vast and peaceful like a cemetery on a clear, cold night. At Christmas there will be my orals to study for, plenty of work to do in the lab, a dozen excuses I can easily give. Later, Linda comes by. She is lovely, unsettling, with bright red hair and skin so pale I think that at any moment she may disappear. Earlier, when she called, she'd told me her period was late.

"Do you think—?" I'd asked.

"I don't know," she'd replied. "No. Probably not."

We make love, and after, she says, "I could stay like this forever." I know I should say, "Me too." Instead, I tell her about Dog. I tell her how I left it at the top of Old Man Hill. I feel her tense, as if she's thinking about the child that may or may not be growing inside her and how I will leave them too. But she relaxes as I go on. I tell her how late that night, I tiptoed out of my room and down the stairs, how I pulled on my coat, boots, and slipped out the door. There, on the sidewalk across the street, sat Dog. His coat was slicked down. His small body shivered. He stood and whined, yet he wouldn't come when I teetered on the opposite curb, clapped my mittens together, called to him. In the end, I'd had to go to him, I told Linda. I'd had to find something tucked away inside me, something enduring and brave that I'd never known was there.

This is the story I tell Linda. By the end, her eyes have closed, and her breathing is slow and even against me. "So it's a happy ending," I tell her even though she doesn't hear. For a second I can almost believe it. I think that if I tell the story often enough, adding to it, drawing out the crucial, climactic scene—me on the curb, teetering, hesitating, Dog on the other side, waiting for me to take this risk—I can will it true, just as my father had willed it true that I would have a brother. I reach over to the nightstand, flick off the lamp, but leave the tank light on. It shines blue as it did the night my father went out looking for Dog. He'd gone first in the car, then on foot, and it was well past midnight when he crept into my room, his boots leaving small, slushy puddles on the carpet, his breath a sickening scrape. He lay Dog in the basket by my bed, covered him with a thick towel, rubbed his damp fur dry. Then, palms raised as if to say, "There. Stay there. Just like that," he backed out of the room, determined, the best he could, the only way he knew how, to make this an ending we could live with.

Lifeguarding

As he turned onto the lake road, a narrow corridor of thickening pines, Duncan said, "My father drowned in this lake."

His voice was conversational, and Joanna wasn't sure she'd heard him right. He looked straight ahead at the road, his eyes not shifting even as he lifted the can of Budweiser from between his knees. The pavement ended. The wheels bounced over ruts and stones. In brief flashes between the pines, Joanna could see Deep Creek, blue like a robin's egg, dotted with sailboats.

"Drowned?" she asked. "How?"

"He stepped off the dock one night." Duncan's tone was still light. He woke up that morning with a mild hangover, but the Budweiser remedy seemed to be working. "It wasn't an accident. He meant to die."

"God," Joanna said, then wished she hadn't, her one puny word shrinking before something so big. Duncan had scarcely mentioned his father before, and she always figured he'd died of a heart attack or stroke, the usual way.

"Did anyone go in after him?" she asked. "Try to save him?"

He shook his head.

"Did he leave a note?"

He shook his head again.

"But why?" Joanna asked, then saw Duncan's face tighten.

"How should I know?" The gravel was back in his voice. "I'm not a damn mind reader."

Joanna counted to herself: *one and two and three.* Only rarely would Duncan snap at her. He always apologized or something close to it before she reached five.

"There's the Randolphs." Gesturing with his beer can at a long pine-shaded drive, he smiled at her. When Duncan smiled, his whole face got into the act. His eyes came on like lamplights. Then he turned serious, lights out. "I can't tell you why," he continued. "I can't tell myself. Maybe he'd had a rotten round of golf. Maybe it was his way of howling at the moon. Like I said, he never left any explanation."

"Your father golfed?" It sounded to Joanna like a neutral topic.

"Yup," he said.

"And you?"

"Nope. Never have, never will."

Joanna and Duncan had lived together for three months, but what she knew about him, she sometimes thought, wouldn't fill a postcard. She knew he'd been born in Prince Frederick. She knew that before Annapolis he'd lived in Boston, Kennebunkport, and (she wasn't sure when or for how long) Bora-Bora. She knew he liked sailboats, hated politics, slept on his right side, did not like to kiss. Now she knew two more things: father drowned himself, does not play golf.

"There's the sailing club," Duncan said, and Joanna bobbed her head as he pointed out this person's house and that, all tucked out of sight behind thick pines. Through her open window drifted smells of burning charcoal and cut grass, settled-down smells that reminded her of Dublin, Ohio, the backyards of the subdivision where she grew up. Her parents had started taking her to swimming lessons at the Dublin YMCA when she was five. By fifteen she was life-guarding, and it seemed to her an impossible task—to deliberately drown. Even if she didn't want them to, her legs would kick and she'd be treading water, a survivor in spite of herself.

Duncan rested the beer can on her knee. "Almost there," he said. Over her knee his fingers drifted. He was working at a marina that summer, scraping barnacles from hulls. His fingers were thick-calloused and rough. It was an odd sensation, Joanna thought—the cool sweat of the can, the fingers dry as tree bark. She pressed back a shudder. She didn't want Duncan to think she believed his family history could be caught like a cold. She didn't want him to think she was

nervous about meeting his mother and brother. She was
looking forward to it; he'd told her so little about them.

"How old were you?" she asked. "When your father died,
I mean."

"Nineteen," Duncan said. "Twenty."

"That must have been hard. Twenty is so young." She
wondered if he had cried, what that would have looked like:
Duncan crying.

He shrugged. "Not so young. Look at you."

Joanna was twenty-two but, everyone said, very mature
and capable for her age. Duncan was thirty-six, and Joanna
believed she loved him, though she was mature enough not
to say so very often. Duncan would only laugh, say, "Do you
know how many times you'll say that in your life? To how
many men? For you, this is practice."

Sometimes she wasn't sure. She'd never felt much of anything for the string of boys she'd gone out with through high
school and college. Those boys liked to talk about themselves, in loud voices, all the time, as if she were a camera
before which they could turn themselves this way and that,
admiringly, lovingly. The last had lips cool and wiggly like
Jell-O. He drove a new Jeep Cherokee, a gift from his insur-
ance-agent dad, said no one had ever understood him.
Duncan was different. He rarely talked about himself, and
when he did, he spoke in sentences stripped down like a boat
in dry dock. He hadn't told Joanna until now that his father

was a suicide, that in his family taking a long walk off a short dock wasn't just a joke. Sometimes at night while he slept, body straight, back to her, she'd press herself to him and wish that by some undiscovered law of physics, their molecules could mingle. Then she could breathe with his lungs, see with his eyes, experience every story he'd never told her.

And all of this, Duncan said, was only practice, like the dives she used to make into the deep end of the YMCA pool: fifteen feet down and then back up, the weighted dummy locked in her elbow, her ribs squeezed, eardrums popped. Practice or not, her body always reacted as if each rescue was real.

"But what about you?" she asked him once. "Is this practice for you?"

"Habit," Duncan said. He touched her hair. "I'm joking," he added. Joking was a habit too.

Duncan had called the house at Deep Creek a cabin, and Joanna pictured the cabin her parents would rent for a week or two every summer on the only lake in Michigan that seemed to have no fish. That cabin had three small rooms with an outhouse in the back, and when it rained (it always did), the roof leaked over the iron cots and mold spread through their suitcases. To Deep Creek she brought Caladryl, her snakebite kit, a fat roll of toilet paper in a plastic baggie to keep it dry. She wasn't expecting the blacktopped drive, landscaped lawn, a real house with two wings and (she'd later learn) five bathrooms. This, she told herself, was why she loved Duncan and his uncommunicative ways. He held so much of his life in reserve so that he could give her these moments, one by one, each a special surprise.

Duncan's mother met them at the front door. Her name was June, and she was a tiny woman, her back curved into a C. On her head perched a large yellow straw hat. Beneath, her hair was pale violet.

"Finally," she said. She took both of Joanna's hands in hers and beamed. Joanna beamed back.

Then she said, "What took you so long, dear? You promised you'd come back in May to help me open the place up."

Joanna glanced at Duncan and told June she was mistaken; this was the first time they'd met.

"You have to speak up," Duncan said. "She's nearly deaf."

"I'm *Joanna,*" she repeated in a loud voice that echoed off the high ceiling and gave her the uncomfortable feeling she was shouting. "I'm *new.*"

"Yes," June said. "Of course."

"You look good, Mom," Duncan said. "Have you been taking your walks?"

June sighed. "Yes. They brought the baby too." She turned back to Joanna. "Do you still play the piano?"

"No," Joanna replied. She shook her head so she wouldn't have to shout. She'd never played the piano in her life. "I'm sorry. I don't."

June looked disappointed, her eyes small and moist like

two wet seeds. "Well. I guess we'll have to join the others on the deck then."

"I should have warned you about her," Duncan said, glancing back at Joanna as they moved through the living room past a great stone fireplace and long armless couches covered in a bumpy turquoise fabric that made Joanna think of the Fifties. She looked but didn't spot a piano. Duncan cupped his mother's elbow to keep her steady—she wore wedgie-looking heels—and though he was speaking in an everyday tone, June didn't seem to hear him.

"In fact," Duncan said, "I should have told you—"

But they were already through the door, onto the deck where Joanna was introduced to Duncan's brother, his cousin, and his cousin's wife, or maybe it was the other way around. From the deck, smooth lawn and a rhododendron-strewn path led down to the water. Half a dozen kids splashed about the dock that bobbed in the wake of a speed-boat. Joanna heard a nearby sound—like "unh-unh." She looked down, saw a fat baby settled like a sugar sack on the smooth boards. The baby was playing with a stick.

"So you're Duncan's new girlfriend," said Cheryl, who was either Duncan's cousin or Duncan's cousin's wife. She had straight blonde hair cut short like a cap. She wore a T-shirt over her swimsuit that said, "Body by Natural Path" and "Certified Product Representative." She patted the chair beside her. When Joanna sat down, she leaned over and whispered, "I want you to know, I'm on your side."

Joanna blinked. Not knowing what else to do, she nodded. At her feet, the baby poked the stick into its triple-chin, said, "Unh-unh-unh." Across the deck, the others went on with their conversation. A speedboat, traveling without lights at night, had slammed into their moored sailboat the week before. They were trying to decide whether to buy a new one, what the cost would be, what each family member should pay.

"Well, Christ." Duncan was speaking to his brother, Ben. "Do you have any idea who the asshole was? Shouldn't he be paying for the boat?"

"If I knew who the asshole was," Ben said, "I'd be talking to him right now, wouldn't I?" Ben was taller than Duncan, not as tan, but otherwise, Joanna thought, they might be twins with the same sandy hair, mirrored sunglasses, and slender hands that could work the complicated rigging of a sailboat with sureness and grace. Today they both wore polo shirts, faded blue, hanging loose on their narrow frames.

"What about insurance?" Duncan asked.

"Uh-oh," Cheryl said, softly, so only Joanna could hear.

"You tell me," Ben replied. He said each word slowly, emphatically: You. tell. me.

"Unh-unh," the baby said. Joanna watched Duncan duck his head.

"I've been busy," he mumbled.

"Yeah. So I see." At that, Ben looked straight at Joanna, and she wished herself, right now, at the bottom of the

YMCA pool. From the shore a child shouted, "Cannonball!" and then there was a noisy splash. June, settled in a chair that made her look doll-small, announced to no one in particular, "I once went for a round-the-world cruise on the *QE-2*, and it was not that expensive. Not as expensive as you might think."

"She did not," Cheryl whispered to Joanna. She patted Joanna's arm. "Don't worry. We didn't bring you here to hit you up for sailboat money. Don't worry about Ben either. He's just pissed off at the world."

Cheryl's fingers remained on her arm, and Joanna felt steadied by her touch. Now and then—like a moment ago with Ben glaring at her with something like hatred or maybe just contempt—it occurred to her that she ought to be spending this summer with six girlfriends in a rented cottage on Cape Cod. She ought to be gearing up for student teaching, like her mom advised, or packing for graduate school like most of her friends who knew no more than she what they wanted to do with their lives. Instead she'd met Duncan, who sprinkled his conversation with little mentions of sea swells and spice islands, who refused to own more than could be stuffed in a sail bag. Cheryl's fingers felt smooth as if her fingerprints had been filed away. Her skin smelled faintly of turpentine. Joanna wondered if she painted.

"What's Natural Path?" she asked.

"A crock of shit. I won't unload that on you either."

At their feet the baby, stick stuck into its chins, rocked

and made wet gurgling sounds. Cheryl reached down, plucked the stick from its fat hands, tossed the stick at Duncan's head.

"Why don't you get your girlfriend a drink," she called, adding, to Joanna, "That is, if you're old enough."

"Oh, I'm old enough," Joanna said quickly, and Cheryl smiled. Except it wasn't exactly a smile but a tugging at the edges of her mouth—as if with wires, Joanna thought, or maybe strings.

Noon arrived, lingered, then moved on without anyone mentioning lunch or naps for the kids. The baby pulled itself beneath the shade of Cheryl's chair and fell asleep, its diapered bottom straight up, its cheek pressed into the boards. Joanna watched the children drag themselves onto the dock, flop about on their bellies like wet seals, then barrel into the water again. One hand on the other, she pressed her palm into her thigh, counted to herself: *one and two and three.* Beside her chair Duncan paused. She shook her head at a second gin-and-tonic. He brought another drink to June, another beer for himself and Ben. Cheryl gave a noisy sigh, then went inside, returned with a can of Bud Lite for herself.

In the next hour Joanna learned that Cheryl was the wife of Duncan's cousin. David was quiet with a dark beard and long slim fingers. In age he fell between Duncan and Ben, who was midway into his forties. The three men stretched out on lawn chairs, shirts shucked, beer cans resting on taut stomachs. Over the top of David's head, Ben and Duncan quietly bickered. Ben, Joanna gathered, was an orthodontist, successful enough but sapped by the financial and emotional demands of two ex-wives, or that's how he saw it. He wanted to know when Duncan was going to behave like an adult.

"How does forty strike you?" Ben asked. "Think you'll grow up then?"

"If growing up means two ex-wives and a string of kids," Duncan replied, "then no, don't count on it."

"Duncan doesn't change," David said. He said this in the same tone he'd use to observe any common, unchallenged fact: the sun rises in the east, the sky is blue. When David returned from inside with another beer, Cheryl tilted hers, empty, upside down. She said, "I might as well not even be here." She also seemed to be pointing out something everyone already knew, and so no one answered her.

"Remember," David said, "the time Duncan stood on the top rail and tried to fly?"

Ben laughed. "Idiot." He turned to Joanna and showed teeth white and straight as piano keys. "Flapping his shirt and drunk as a skunk, saying, 'Look at me, I can fly!' Broke his ankle on landing."

Ben reached over, flicked Duncan's ear hard enough to make Joanna flinch. "Idiot," he said. "Just like the old man."

"Watch it," Duncan said.

Cheryl whispered, "Their father was a drunk. A suicide too."

"I know," Joanna said. She was glad Duncan had told her the story of his father, even if it was not so much a story as the promise of one. He was like one of her young swimmers, skittish and afraid, while she waited knee-deep in the pool, very patient and very still.

"From what I understand," Cheryl whispered, "he did it quietly, while everyone was inside watching TV, their dinners in their laps. I think that's why no one ever mentions food around here. They've got this idea it can be fatal."

At that, she rose, headed inside, then returned with a tray piled with sandwiches and brown-spotted bananas for the kids around the dock. Joanna watched the kids reach up out of the water, pluck food from the tray until it was empty. *Wait half an hour after eating before you swim,* she thought automatically. Duncan stopped by her chair again, pointed at her empty glass. Joanna shook her head. *One and two and three,* she counted to herself, just in case the need should arise for CPR. Cheryl returned to her chair and began to tell her everything Duncan had not. Four of the kids were products of Ben's marriages, in his custody every other weekend; the other two plus the baby belonged to her and David. David ran the printing company in Bethesda that Duncan's father had started and that neither brother would have anything to do with, Ben wanting to make more money and Duncan, apparently, less.

"And here I am," Cheryl said, "the certified product representative for Nature's Way, jars of sheep fat creams I wouldn't put on a dog. I was a painter when I met David. Well, I worked in a T-shirt shop, air-brushed sailboat designs, beach scenes. These days my hands can't take the rest of me seriously, not even enough to paint T-shirts."

David, she said, didn't have a head for business, June was losing her marbles, and summer came too late to Deep Creek Lake, the water knife-cold through August when everyone packed up their cars and drove back to where they really lived. Words rushed from her like water from a pipe, and Joanna thought it must have been a very long time since anyone had said, "Cheryl, what do you think?" David, Joanna observed, hadn't looked their way once that afternoon and lately, neither had Duncan. Every now and then, one would stand, rub his eyes, then stomp inside and return. *Two and three and four.* Now Joanna tallied beers. Across from her, June dozed, her snores whispering like pine boughs, her hat fallen away. At the pop of a beer, she'd startle, look about with her wet-seed eyes, glance down at her drink. It was speckled with tiny drowned gnats, but maybe she couldn't see that because she would take a sip, then doze once more.

At one point she blinked her eyes open and said to Joanna, "Did I miss it?"

Joanna looked at her.

"The recital. You didn't play already, did you?"

"No," Joanna said.

Duncan added, "Mom, this is *Joanna.* She's *new.*"

"She's thinking of this girl who came last summer," Cheryl explained. "She was very young like you. I can't remember her name, but Duncan met her in Boston. She was studying at the conservatory. You're in school, aren't you? What are you studying?"

"Anthropology," Joanna replied, vaguely. She was thinking of a girl who not only played the piano but studied it too. She had liked to believe that Duncan's old girlfriends had first names ending in heart-dotted "i"s. She did not like to think that one at least ought to have been taken seriously and was not. Duncan, naturally, had never mentioned her.

"But I'm done with school," she added. "I graduated in May."

"What are your plans?"

Beneath Cheryl's chair, the baby roused and after a few "unh-unh"s, it made one loud, insistent cry. Cheryl lifted it to her lap and in what seemed like a single motion she raised her shirt, undid her suit, tucked the baby to her breast. Joanna shifted her eyes to the shore. The kids lined up on the dock. One by one they marched off the end, their feet breaking the water with hardly a splash, their bodies slipping quietly, eerily out of sight. They lined up again. It was some kind of game.

When Joanna had moved in with Duncan, they'd agreed it was temporary—"Kind of like summer camp," she had said cheerily. She'd been surprised by the offer and relieved not to be spending another dreary Ohio summer lifeguarding at the pool as if she were still sixteen, her mother dropping reminders that, thanks to the second mortgage and assorted loans, Joanna's education was something they'd be paying off for years to come. In his apartment Duncan had only one saucepan, but when he asked her if they should buy more, she'd replied, with a great deal of maturity, "Really, there's no point." She had a summer job with the Red Cross, teaching first-aid and water safety. From work she brought plastic-wrapped disaster meal kits so they could have boil-in-the-bag chicken à la king or beef stew for supper. Most nights, though, Duncan telephoned her from Marmaduke's, his voice half-drowned by the shouts of his buddies: "Hey Joanna" and "Get down here, girl." Duncan never mentioned having plans beyond this summer, and by now Joanna had learned to let the future skim ahead, pulling her along like a hapless dinghy. It was easy simply to sit on this deck, her mind occupied with gathering small facts or rehearsing the steps for CPR, and it took a great effort to summon up the usual answers for Cheryl's question: maybe teaching, maybe graduate school, or maybe . . . unless . . . it depends. . . .

Then she heard Duncan say, "I've been thinking about Australia." He spoke to David and Ben, his eyes closed, body stretched out on the lawn chair. "I'm thinking I'll head there next month after the marina lays off. In Australia, they'll just be starting summer."

Joanna sat forward in her chair. Cheryl perked up too. Ben made a noise that sounded like disgust.

"That'll be good for Joanna," Cheryl said. On her face she

wore the pulled-string smile. "Australia is a good place for anthropologists."

"Oh, Joanna's got other plans," Duncan said. He opened his eyes and regarded her as if waiting for her to agree. Joanna didn't say anything. At that moment, her tongue was stitched to her teeth.

"Jesus, Duncan," Ben said. "That's the fucking bottom of the world."

"I think," David said evenly, "that's the idea."

June clasped her knees, her head turning this way and that, trying to catch it all. "You'll like Austria," she told Joanna. "I did."

"She's never been to Austria," Cheryl whispered.

"*Mom,*" Duncan said loudly. "I'm going to *Australia,* and Joanna *isn't* going with me. She's got *other* plans."

He looked at her again, and Joanna felt hot prickles rise on her face. It occurred to her that in her bag with the Caladryl and snakebite kit, she'd forgotten to pack sunscreen. It occurred to her too that she could not breathe and Cheryl was watching, nodding, as if something had been made clear.

In the kitchen Joanna made a fresh gin-and-tonic for June, then bent over the sink and splashed water on her face. The kitchen was dark and cool like a shady cove. She could feel herself surfacing, the pounding in her ears start to ebb. The clock over the stove said it was four, and Duncan, she thought, should be ready to go soon. She opened the refrigerator, scanned the shelves: two bottles of tonic, half a jug of milk, a rotting cut lime. She should find something for them to eat, bring a tray of sandwiches out on the deck, show everyone she was unperturbed by talk of Australia, none of it news to her.

The kitchen door swung open, and Duncan ambled in. He stopped next to her and peered into the refrigerator. Joanna noticed he kept his arms pressed to his sides, taking care not to touch her.

"No beer," he said. He reached for a bottle of tonic.

"You have to work tomorrow," Joanna said.

"Yeah."

"You have to drive home too."

"Your point?"

Duncan's car was a stick shift, and though they'd talked about Joanna learning to drive it, they'd never gotten around to lessons. The week before they'd left it in the parking lot of a 7-Eleven half a block from Marmaduke's. She hadn't kept count that night, and when she asked Duncan if he was okay, his fist clenched the keys. Two minutes later he'd guided the car into the 7-Eleven lot, cut the motor, pulled the brake, and then, as if there were nothing odd about this, laid his head in her lap. "Sleep?" he'd said. "Time to sleep?" She'd actually sat there, with Duncan nestling against her thighs, for some time, maybe an hour, even though she'd nursed just one watery margarita through the evening and was perfectly steady to walk into the 7-Eleven and call a cab.

"I just thought," Joanna said now, "since you've had so many beers, and since it's such a long drive—"

"So many beers?" Duncan stood at the counter, his back to her, his movements very exact as he measured a double shot, flipped it into his glass.

"Well, six, including the one you had on the drive here."

"So you can count. Good for you. Maybe that'll get you a job." Now he sounded an awful lot like Ben.

In the doorway Cheryl appeared, bent at the waist and holding the baby by its wrists as it tested out standing on unsteady legs.

"Unh-unh," the baby said. It tried to reach a plump foot forward.

"Diaper change," Cheryl said.

Duncan nodded, stepped around her, and vanished outside. Scooping the baby up, Cheryl moved to the counter. She used a cloth diaper and pins, something Joanna had never seen before. Her hands moved nimbly. The baby's face reddened as if to cry. Then it changed its mind, blew spit-bubbles instead.

"I really am on your side," Cheryl said. "After Duncan's gone, I want you to come visit me. I want us to be friends. It's hard. Getting to know people and then having them drop right out of your life."

"Like last summer's girl," Joanna said. She wondered that she felt so little. She'd been expecting more, a great well of grief.

"Exactly," Cheryl replied. She rattled a small toy over the baby's face and smiled down at it. "She said she'd write, then didn't, and now I can't even remember her name."

"Remember whose name?" Duncan was back. Joanna felt his hand touch her waist, then stay there.

"Who are you talking about?" he asked.

"No one you know," Cheryl replied.

He pointed to the gin-and-tonic Joanna had made for June. "Mom's looking for her drink," he said.

"The ice is melted," Joanna told him. His hand stayed against her. As one finger traced the curve from her ribs to hip and back, she thought it would not be so bad. In the next week or two, however long it took them to make their separate plans, they would be solicitous, polite. They might even make love—but carefully, as if each were stamped with the word *fragile*. Maybe Duncan had been right. Maybe this was good practice for future relationships at their sorry ends.

"Wait," she told him. "I'll fix her another."

"No, no, I'll get it." He took the glass from her fingers, smiled at her but with his mouth only, no lamplights coming on. "You relax," he said.

"Well." Cheryl lifted the baby. "I should leave you two to talk."

"Talk?" Duncan asked. His hand dropped from Joanna's waist. He reached for the gin.

"Talk about what?" Joanna said.

It might have ended like that, Joanna would think, later, whenever she and Duncan returned to Deep Creek. So easily it might have ended exactly as they'd planned, and she would have gone on to practice love with other men, the rhythms of falling in and falling out just as natural to her as treading water. But later David had pulled out a pipe, and Ben had suggested the garage out of sight of the kids who were critical of that sort of thing, and there in the garage, while they were getting high, Duncan had found his father's golf clubs.

From the deck Joanna could hear them arguing. It was getting dark, and Cheryl had put the baby to bed, was calling in the kids. They dragged themselves up the path, too tired to protest. They marched, dripping water, smelling of muck, past Joanna's chair.

"Fuck you," she heard Duncan say. He sounded drunk.

"Those were Dad's," Ben said. "By rights they go to me. I don't want you touching them. You don't even play golf."

"Fuck you." He sounded very drunk. Loaded.

"Idiot."

"Hey, relax. Don't fight." That was David, the peacemaker, or maybe he was stoned.

"Is it Friday?" June asked. She still sat across from Joanna.

Her hat was back in place. Cheryl had turned the porch light out to keep the bugs away, and June's face was a blank shadow, a strange, featureless egg.

"It's Sunday," Joanna said.

"Sunday," June repeated, pushing herself up. "Ed Sullivan. I think I'll go in."

Joanna watched her go, not knowing how to explain that Ed Sullivan had not aired in years. Then she got up too and followed the arguing voices into the garage. When she walked in, the bickering stopped. The garage smelled of wet Styrofoam, sweetened by pot. It was completely quiet except for the flicker of moths' wings against the bare overhead bulb, the scuff of her bare feet on cement. Ben and David stood against a wall. In the center of the garage stooped Duncan. He held a putter in his hands, its tip lining up with a bright red golf ball on the floor. He seemed to be crying, without sound, his chest moving up and down like a bobber. Joanna had the strange sensation they'd all been poised like this for several minutes, or maybe several years.

"Idiot," Ben said, in the same voice he might use to say "Brother" or "Love."

"Hey, Duncan," David said drowsily. "Here's Joanna. How about you let her put you to bed?"

From Duncan's hands Joanna eased the putter. When he asked, "Where are we going?" the words slid together as if to dance.

"Nowhere," she said. "Inside." She heard the TV then and June's voice wavering high above it, "What are they saying?" Joanna corrected herself. "Outside. For a walk."

Duncan followed along on shaky legs. At the end of the dock, they could go no farther. Joanna sat cross-legged on the damp boards. Duncan curled up on his side. He put his head in her lap, and she stroked his cheek. The fist that had gripped the golf club loosened, unfolded. Behind them Cheryl appeared. She hesitated, scratching her shin with a bare toe. Joanna smiled and patted the boards beside her.

"Muggy tonight," Cheryl observed. She slapped a mosquito on her neck. Beside her she set a baby monitor, and Joanna listened to the sounds of soft, steady breathing. The dock bobbed gently. Out on the lake, far in the distance, a lone speedboat buzzed. Joanna tensed, remembering the speedboat that had slammed through the moored sailboat. Then she relaxed. Nothing was going to happen. Nothing like that. From the water mist rose like a curtain.

"Did you know," Cheryl said, "that if you row out onto the lake and shout, you can hear a double echo? Two times your voice comes back to you."

"Really," Joanna said. "We should try it sometime." Suddenly it seemed possible they would do just that, one calm night beneath a new moon. Cheryl yawned, lay back, then pillowed her head with her hands, as if to stay there for the night or until she heard the baby start to cry. Joanna felt her own heart settle down too, her breathing drift toward sleep. *One and two and three.* Later, she knew, she would learn much more: how to rig a sailboat, coax beers from Duncan's hand, how to smile benignly when he spoke of far-away places he'd never go. Duncan would tell Joanna he loved her. He would say he meant it, he did: this time he really was sunk. Joanna would believe him, even if he never said it again, or never in that way. To June she would no longer need to shout, *I'm Joanna* and *I'm new.* She would grow familiar. She would grow old. And maybe one night the three of them—she, Cheryl, Duncan too—would row to the middle of the lake. They would shout foolishness at the sky, then wait for their voices to come back twice. As if astonished, as if this had never happened before, they would look at one another, say, "Listen. Do you hear it? There it is."

Texas Sounds Like
an Easy Place to Leave

Amber can't say she knew the woman. She didn't even learn her name until the day the woman died, though she would see her, the husband too, mornings when Amber stepped outside to pack Steven and Ron Junior off to school.

Amber always marches her sons down the driveway. She places her palms square on their bulky packs and gives them a push, gentle but firm, in the clear direction of school. Off they go, a little bent beneath their loads—they look like soldiers except they are humping history books, gym shoes, pudding cups—eyes squinting against a gritty breeze. They do not need their mother to point the way. They were born with the interstate highway system mapped in their brains, or that's what Ron, Amber's husband, likes to joke.

"We're more reliable than Triple A," Ron says. "Drop us anyplace, anyplace at all, and we'll point you the way to Route 80." At the occasional backyard cookout, especially those with open coolers on the concrete patios, Ron urges anyone who'll listen to blindfold him, drive him out in the country, dump him off. So far, no one's taken him up on it, though Amber doesn't doubt that as long as he can pull himself more or less upright, he'll find his way back to whatever place they are calling home. Ron and the boys are like homing pigeons, Amber thinks. Except they are more adaptable, one roost the same as any other.

Lately, though, Ron Junior has shown a tendency to stray and Steven, admiration for his older brother overriding all good sense, to follow. Every morning Amber lines them up, their bodies stiff but obedient. Every morning she tries to steer them straight. "Ronny," she says, "you're responsible" or "Ron Junior, you know the way." One morning Ron Junior slipped out the door while Steven was finishing his cereal and Amber was pouring a second cup of coffee. She packed Steven into the car, drove back and forth between home and school, searching out every imaginable route except the one cutting through the littered field by the old wastewater treatment plant. This field's high, rough grass hides ticks, broken beer bottles, and dirty hypodermics, or so Amber, who reads the local paper and watches the TV news, has reason to believe. From the littered field to the middle school it is a mad dash across four lanes of state highway. (Drunken drivers, Amber thinks. Truckers strung out on crystal meth.) Ron Junior took this forbidden route just once, for which his father gave him a stern talking-to. He'd been grounded for one weekend, prohibited from video games and cable TV. For her own lapse in vigilance,

Amber drank no coffee for two days. She carried her headache like her boys carry books on their backs.

Most mornings the woman would be outside too, packing the trunk of a Hyundai two-door. It was her car; the husband's was a red Mustang that sat by the curb, "For Sale" soaped across the windshield, redone each time it rained. Grass grew in high tufts around the wheels where the lawn mower couldn't go.

"What is this—West Virginia?" Ron complained. He doesn't like cars parked in yards, even fancy new Mustangs. He says it makes a neighborhood look cheap. He says it brings down the value of their home too. Of all the places Amber and Ron have lived, West Virginia isn't one of them, and in Ron's mind, West Virginia is what it means to hit bottom. Amber refrains from noting that most likely West Virginia is a lovely state with low taxes and an affordable public university. She understands that it matters to Ron, when things turn bad, to picture someplace worse than where they are.

Within a few days the Mustang was joined by a snowblower and a John Deere riding mower. They didn't have "For Sale" signs on them. There were enough snowblowers, riding mowers, and ATVs sitting by curbs up and down the street for this to be implied. Now the grass grew up everywhere. When an animal got into the garbage, the woman and her husband left it like that, cans on their sides, discarded toilet paper rolls and bloody meat wrappers scattered and snagged on weeds.

"Hillbillies," Ron said, though only for a couple of days. Then he got laid off too and stopped going outdoors where the neighbors' yard could offend him.

The woman had been a music teacher. Amber had picked this up somewhere along the way. Amber always makes a point of learning who lives around them and by what means. It matters to know that the chained dog around the block isn't standing guard over nightly drug deals, that the varsity cheerleader arrested for shoplifting has since found God and always wears a bracelet she consults like a Ouija board to remind her that, among other things, Jesus would never steal. Amber reads the crime blotter every week—domestic disturbances, DUIs—and keeps an eye out for potential trouble. This used to make Ron laugh. You're turning into a nosy housewife, he would say. Ron never reads the newspaper, tunes into the news only for sports. There is so much he does not know. There is a duplex on the corner, occupied by a steady rotation of women, usually single, usually with children, a different car parked out front just about every night. In the blank parking lot of what used to be the K-Mart, Amber spies a pack of kids, hardly older than Ron Junior, with spiky black hair and spooky pale faces. Who do such children belong to, Amber wonders. When she asks Ron Junior, he claims not to know, and why, Amber thinks, should he?

Amber and Ron's circle of friends is composed of other

couples whose children match Ron Junior and Steven in age and attraction to sports. It never included the couple across the street whose children were grown. They were thought to have lived in the neighborhood for a long while and so belonged to another generation, one with different ideas about friendship and stability. Amber and her friends greet one another on the sidewalk with bright smiles, cocked heads, and wagging fingers. They talk about their sons, daughters, and, occasionally, crafts. At parties and backyard barbeques—hosted by younger couples who haven't yet learned to ration themselves—Amber drinks no more than one glass of white zinfandel and quietly declines further intimacy. No, not a movie, not even a date for coffee. She is so busy. She is always very busy. There is settling in and unpacking, learning the way to the grocery store, choosing a church (typically Presbyterian, undemanding, unremarkable). Then there is repacking, arranging final meter reads, taking half a second to hand Steven a book *(New Places, New Friends)*, to ask Ron Junior how he's doing (sullen scowl, no response). When Amber's mother visits—it doesn't matter which state, in what relation to Route 80—she always asks why no one plants a tree, why Amber can't at least put in some shrubs. When Amber's mother looked across the street where the woman lived (this was before, when the yard was still well kept), she admired the stone goose on the front steps that the woman dressed according to the day's forecast—a pink sundress and parasol, a yellow slicker and cap.

He didn't pause for confirmation and gave Amber no chance to point out what about her raised ranch might stand out from the rest: the new wallpaper border in the dining room, for example, or the mini-greenhouse window above the kitchen sink. The realtor spoke rapidly, as if from a script. "We'll be by tonight between five and eight. Expect to list at one-thirty-five, less if you really want it to move."

"Well," said the woman, moving another foot forward, sidestepping a bit of trash—a flattened Hungry Man frozen dinner box, a greasy piece of foil. She looked at Amber as if there was something she'd like to add. "Good luck" perhaps, and, given that for-sale signs had sprung up like dandelions, "You'll need it." Amber waited. Her head was still cocked, her smile starting to smart. The woman clasped her hands, and Amber had a sudden panicky feeling. She and Ron had lived on this street for nearly two years, a record for them, and she and this woman had never exchanged a word, let alone a covered casserole. It seemed a little late now.

"My name's Darcy," the woman finally offered. "If there's anything you need or anything I can do." As if she was from the Welcome Wagon.

It wouldn't have killed Amber. This is what she thinks, later. "Nice to meet you, Darcy," Amber could have said, and "No, we're fine. Is there anything we can do for you?" She could have asked after Darcy's husband, told her it was the same with Ron for the first few days, as he sat and stewed and then, sometimes, unexpectedly boiled over, scaring the bejesus out of her and the boys, but just once or twice and only for the first few days, until he pulled himself together. She could have counseled Darcy on the importance of making sure that the downsized husband sticks to a routine: shower, shave, clean underwear, a shirt. Make a list. Ask him to do one thing each day—solve the mystery of the sweating toilet, replace that hard-to-reach lightbulb—that will demonstrate how skilled and necessary he still is. She really should write such ideas up for one of those magazines offering seventy-five bucks for helpful household tips. She could have let Darcy in on the usefulness of imagining that in West Virginia, things were probably worse. Slowly her painful smile would relax. Her head would sit up straight on her neck the way God had intended it to. Such a conversation would have cost Amber nothing, could have saved Darcy her life. Amber considers this, every now and then or, if truth be told, more often than that. Then she shakes it off. They have never lived anywhere long enough to make a difference. "I'm sorry," Amber says to petitioners and politicians who knock at their door. "We don't really live here."

Bill was the husband's name. Bill and Darcy Rausch. Before the layoffs, Amber sometimes spotted him, coming and going from work. His wardrobe never varied—chinos, checkered shirt (short-sleeved in summer), an indifferently knotted tie. Office drone, said Ron, who did time-studies in the plant and did not fraternize—his word—with behind-the-desk types even though Ron's work uniform, minus the tie, was exactly the same, as were his at-home habits. Saturdays all the husbands on the street mounted their John Deeres and mowed the grass. On appropriate holidays, they hung out flags. Other than the Mustang, there was nothing remarkable about Bill Rausch. Amber had not seen him head for the woods, shotgun in hand, as Ron did as soon as late autumn arrived. He had never seemed like the sportsman type.

There are those, later on, who swear they saw the signs, that showy red Mustang for starters. Some claim they're lucky Bill Rausch didn't take it out on everyone. Others tell tales of stirred-up voices, crashing vases, desperate calls to 911. But Amber has read the blotter faithfully. She's never seen an entry, never spotted a cruiser in the Rausches' drive. Any loud noise could only have been the TV.

"I heard she drove him to it," announces Ron Junior at supper one night.

"Don't say that," Amber replies. She keeps her voice calm. She is aware of doing this, of making her voice steady, flat.

"Listen to your mother," Ron adds, between mouthfuls.

"How come, if it's true? I heard she was such a lard-butt—"

"Shut your trap," Amber says. With that, she feels them—Ron, Steven, Ron Junior—looking at her. This is not the kind of thing Amber typically says or has ever said. She concentrates on cutting her green beans, one by one, neatly in half. They are the frozen kind, already cut into bite-sized rectangles that she now turns into tiny squares. She tries to swallow a feeling, hot and inappropriate, but it sticks in her throat and starts to swell. She wishes Ron, Steven, and Ron Junior would stop looking at her, would just go away, disappear—vamoose! She can almost feel it, what it would be to just shoot out of there—free! unfettered!—throwing off the dead weight of her husband, the sticky hands of two boys grabbing at her neck.

Ron Junior is silent. Then he continues. "At school they said there was so much gore, swear to God, one of the cops blew chunks—"

When Amber reaches over and slaps her son, hard, right smack across his filthy mouth, it is herself she surprises most of all. Her hand stings, and she stares at it, amazed. Look at what that hand did, she thinks, without even her say-so. And what words—*filthy mouth, stupid brat, I'll show you*—have just detonated in her brain? She sets the offending hand back in her lap, takes a breath, then looks up and around. Somehow she's hoping that no one, not even Ron Junior, has noticed what her hand just did. Steven is wide-eyed. Ron has set down his fork. For the first time in months, in years, he regards her without need (she is his rock, his compass, their foundation, roof, and walls) and without blame (if he'd never married her, if she hadn't gotten pregnant, her fault). He regards her instead with simple, naked astonishment at this rip in her otherwise implacable response to every kind of challenge: broken arms, burnt pork chops, bounced checks and collection calls. Ron Junior refuses to return her look. He gazes at some point just beyond her, a future in which, because of that slap, he is freed from having to follow her direction. In this future, Amber will tell him, "You're responsible," and he will reply, "You can go to hell."

Finally Ron clears his throat and tells the boys to eat up. Steven crosses his arms over his chest and kicks at the table leg, and Amber wonders if, later, when she tries to take him into her lap, he will even let her, will ever let her do such a thing again. Ron Junior rubs his jaw.

"Jesus, Mom," he says. He seems to know that he can say that now. Jesus. Shit. Christ. Goddamn. "What was that for?"

"Just drop it," his father says. "We didn't even know those people. We got no business talking about them."

But Amber wants to talk about them, about Darcy and about Bill, turning them into people they knew, a story they can tell. "There were these people across the street, the last place we lived. We weren't close but . . ." The story will gently set off to one side the question of what expression had crossed Darcy's face that morning when Amber turned away, off to answer a phone that had not rung. Amber hadn't looked back, so she didn't know if Darcy had been hurt, offended, or if Amber's rebuff had registered at all. It seems likely now that Amber had been the last—or if you want to put a fine point on it, next to last—person to have seen Darcy alive.

"Did you see or hear anything suspicious?" asked the one police officer who was sent, perfunctorily, to investigate, even though the case was pretty much closed.

No, Amber told him. She decided not to say, though she wasn't sure why, that she had taken notice of the Hyundai. It had spent the rest of the morning in the driveway, its trunk open and only half-packed. She had poured another cup of coffee, paused at the door on the way down to pack up more boxes. She hadn't actually heard anything. Who would with UPS trucks chugging down the street, a shortcut to the plant, and it had been garbage day besides. But she had noticed the car. She had thought it odd. She had even thought, just for a second, that she ought to take a closer look.

Just about everyone Amber has ever known would understand—if she would tell them, which she will not—why she marched herself downstairs and went back to packing instead. Just about everyone Amber has known, as an adult anyway, has also moved from one place to the next: layoffs in Rochester, a brief boom in Racine. Everything depends on sticking with what's familiar. Before each closing, they stay at a Holiday Inn, eat at the Denny's, memorize the numbers for a house in a subdivision that looks exactly like the one they just left where the streets were named for the all the varieties of conifers or sometimes flowers or birds. Each house has a slim, hopeful sapling cabled out front. They settle in like the sod rolled out to give them an instant lawn. On

the sidewalks Amber meets other mothers with bright conversation, strained smiles, and frequent migraines. There
was a time when Amber had let herself think of such women
as lifelong friends, and, worse still, had allowed Ron Junior
to get too close to another little boy. This was nine or ten
years ago—in Muncie, Indiana—and still Ron Junior tells
her that he has never gotten over it and will never forgive her
for failing to remember the little boy's last name. Just recently when Amber told him to please pick up his room, that she
was not going to ask again, he looked up from his computer. He said he was in the midst of an Internet search—
"Robby," "Robert," and "Muncie, Indiana." He said he'd
received eleven thousand hits and this was going to take a
while.

Amber can't tell Ron she's worried about their son. "You
think it's my fault," Ron will say, and then, "I'm a failure" and
"You'd be better off without me." No, no, Amber will have to
reply. You've misunderstood and besides, things are looking
up. They've figured out their next move. To Tyler, Texas,
contract work, no benefits, but still, it's a job. She says to
Steven, "Think of the new friends you'll make," and Steven,
looking and sounding more like Ron Junior by the minute,
answers, "Really, Mom, what's the point?" Her sons have
learned to pick up and let go of friends like a ball in play.
Amber herself has learned to collect nothing that can't be
carted off in a basket to the Goodwill. Scrapbooks and sam-
plers, tole-painted angels and flags with hopeful messages

like *America* and *Believe:* out it all goes. The plant manager
down in Texas has told Ron that perhaps—if things pick up
and Ron works out—something permanent could come
along. But if it doesn't, so what? That's what Amber tells Ron.
Texas sounds like an easy place to leave. She has learned to
make every place easy to leave.

Though she is amazed, sometimes, at what refuses to be
shed. A little wooden footbridge over a singing creek in
Gadsden, Alabama. There it is, stuck in her brain, refusing to
budge, along with the memory of an unexpected thrill that
had surged through her body as their minivan crossed the
Missouri and passed beneath a sign welcoming them to
Nebraska and *The Good Life,* which they had lived for exactly ten-and-a-half months. There is always so much clutter—
the memory of what it was like to have one good girlfriend,
a naive dream about escaping each day to an office job and
wearing two-toned pumps, a not-so-long-ago party, one of
Ron's coworkers drawing her into a hall closet for a long and
beery kiss—so much she can't get rid of, though she continues to try. It is, after all, only her sunny, finger-wagging
refusal of attachments that keeps her boys from getting their
hearts broken over and over again, that keeps them from
growing into bitter, dependent men unable to adjust to
change and disappointment. Her constancy, her imper-
turbability—this is also, she believes, what keeps her husband from putting a gun to his head like Bill Rausch did
right after he'd pulled the trigger on his wife. It happened,

Amber gathers, shortly after she'd left Darcy at the drive-way's end.

It is, for a while, the talk of the neighborhood. For a while, in fact, their street is like a real neighborhood with men calling to one another over the buzz of mowers, women gathering to talk after waving children off to school. Amber sticks to packing, now and then pausing to look up facts—population, gross income per capita, crime and divorce rates—for Tyler, Texas. From Ron and the boys she picks up bits of the story from across the street, though there is little beyond the spare newspaper facts she can credit as true. Everyone swears they saw it coming, though in the end it appears no one had known Bill Rausch any more than they know each other. Ron reports on the lack of a note, rumors of third parties and foul play. Steven comes home from school with ghastly tales of body parts sprayed across two rooms.

"Enough," Amber tells Ron.

"Don't tell tales," she admonishes Steven. She would say the same to Ron Junior except he no longer comes straight home from school. He has taken to wearing nothing but black and something around his neck that looks like it prop-erly belongs on a dog. She never knows just where he might be.

Amber herself has no time for women out on the side-walk. She is busy, busy, busy with the truck to rent, addresses to change, minimums to send for their pile of credit cards. Finally the realtor calls; someone is interested in taking a look. Amber is supposed to be out—she's run out of boxes and tape; there is always more than she expects—but the agent comes early, then glowers as if Amber is the one with the faulty sense of time.

"What's the neighborhood like?" the woman asks her. She is part of a couple, young. He is out back, inspecting the questionable foundation, frowning at the grass. She has already decided that Ron Junior's room would make the best nursery. Amber can't imagine where they have come from, what they are doing. Perhaps they exist in a parallel universe, one in which this town actually has jobs, a resuscitated downtown.

"It's a nice neighborhood," Amber says. "Very quiet."

"We looked at the house across the street too," the young woman says.

Amber glances at the agent. The agent takes the woman's elbow, a little roughly, Amber thinks. He points out the good wear left in the hall carpet. The woman looks back. "It's just like this one, isn't it?"

"Yes," Amber agrees. "It's exactly the same."

When she thinks about Darcy, she wonders if it happened by design. Was she just about ready to shut the trunk but then Bill called her back into the house? Or had Darcy gone back for forgotten kazoos, Bill, having decided that his own life was a failure, not worth living, figuring on the spot that neither was hers. One afternoon, maybe a week after it had happened, Amber walked into her own house, looked up, saw Ron at the top of the stairs. He was still in his undershirt and shorts. It had been days since he'd shaved. He looked like he'd been waiting for her.

"It's about time," he said.

He started down the stairs, moving towards her, getting closer, his eyes steady on her face.

"I can't find—hey! Jesus, Amber, what's the matter with you?"

But this had happened only once, and immediately after, Amber reflected that she had not been so much frightened as startled; for one instant she had not recognized this man with stubbled face and grayed undershirt who was speaking her name, who was moving towards her down the stairs, who reaches for her, now and then, across the empty middle of the bed. It's only Ron, she tells herself, just like she tells herself that it's only Ron Junior and his friends, when she drives past a cluster of slouching, crowlike kids. She tries to recall the flash of gratitude she'd felt the one afternoon when Ron Junior, without shifting his eyes from a video game, said to her, out of the blue, "I s'pose I love you, Mom." She tries to conjure up the shivery sensation of her husband's light breath against her bare neck. What comes to her instead is the image of Ron's shotgun. It's propped at this very moment against the back door, unloaded, he always says, though she has her doubts. She has, on principle, never touched it, but even so, in this moment, she can feel its heft. She marvels at the dull metal's surprising warmth, the firm but gentle squeeze required by the trigger, a sharp kick against her shoulder, the future exploding before her very eyes. Then, quietly, deliberately, Amber puts this thought away, off to the side with the other unmentionable things she always means to leave behind, like wet, beery kisses from strange men in closets or the nearly overwhelming desire she'd frequently felt, years ago, to softly ease her sons' small heads beneath the bathtub's water line.

Soon enough, one by one, all the houses on this street will be sold, foreclosed, or simply abandoned, by the necessity of another job in another state, to the realtor who starts them all at one-thirty-five and then goes down from there. It might be ten years or more before this town comes back. That's what Amber thinks as they pull away; it is what she thinks every time they pull away. By then, Darcy and Bill, their story in all its versions, will be long gone, not even history. As for Amber, Ron, and their boys, Texas is not so bad, though it doesn't look like they'll have reason to stay.

Sweet Maddy

On prom night Maddy and I sat on my front porch and watched the cars pull in, clumsy Detroit-built cars in somber colors like copper and gray. Their doors popped open, and slick-haired boys tumbled out. To their chests they clutched corsage boxes like tiny white coffins. We noticed they stuck to the front walks, as if they were too fine to track through grass, as if they weren't Stevie, Winston, Robby Junior—boys we'd known since before we could speak.

It was a warm night, and the azalea bushes around my front porch were in full, shocking-pink bloom. My mother always winced at those azaleas and their aggressive color, as if others might think them sassy, maybe even obscene. At that moment she stood with Mrs. Jackson from next door, apologizing for them.

"It's the acid in the soil," she said. "Nothing helps, not even the fertilizer the man at Dan's Nursery up in Elyria swore would make them bloom a nice, quiet pink."

Maddy and I looked at each other and rolled our eyes. Then Maddy nudged me, pointed across the street. There, beneath a papery birch, Mr. Bowman had lined up his daughter Lynnette and her date, Stevie Blumenshein, as if for a firing squad. Lynnette wore a powder-blue gown that matched Stevie's tux and that Maddy and I both knew she'd bought at the Second-Time-Around. She batted a hand in front of her nose while Mr. Bowman barked, "Smile! Hold still!"

"Oh-oh, a bee," Maddy mimicked. "Save me, Stevie, save me."

I grinned, then suggested we shout across the street that Lynnette was wearing the same gown Roberta Myers had worn the year before, when she lost her virginity and got pregnant all in the same eventful evening. Roberta always paraded Baby—that's what she'd named it, Baby—around in its carriage. Roberta was fat now with stringy hair, and Baby had a bald head and flat raisin eyes. The rest of the high-school girls cooed as if they hoped the same thing would happen to them. Maddy and I agreed we'd rather be buried alive—the most terrible thing we could imagine, at that time.

Just then, Mrs. Jackson shouted up to us, "Maddy! Jane! How come you girls ain't dressed yet? Darlene's been ready for hours."

Maddy and I sunk back on our elbows. We'd thought the azalea bushes kept us hidden from view.

"They're not going," my mother explained.

"*Not going?*" Each word sounded like a gunshot, and we scooted on our butts back into the shadows. I imagined Mr. Bowman had heard and was turning around to stare. I imagined Stevie and Lynnette catching sight of us, smirking.

"You're shitting me," Mrs. Jackson said.

My mother frowned, just briefly, then smoothed her face into impassive pleasantness once more. She'd grown up in what she thought of as a moderately prosperous, polite family in Shaker Heights. She'd never gotten used to the way people in these parts said things like "You're shitting me." Now and then Mrs. Jackson showed up with a purplish skid-mark across one cheek, and my mother would avert her eyes, argue later with my father about moving to Shaker Heights, never mind the cost. And what made her think Shaker Heights was any different? my father would ask. Money might give people nice manners, he would say, but it can't make them kind.

Mrs. Jackson moved to the front walk to get a better look at Maddy and me. "How come you girls ain't going to prom?" she called.

"Because, Mrs. Jackson," Maddy said, "we're not sluts."

At that I sat up straight, sucked in my breath so hard it hurt my gut. Mrs. Jackson peered at Maddy, cocked her head, and said, "Come again?" My mother bit her lip, and I wondered if she bit back a hoot of laughter. Then, as if nothing at all had been said, she took Mrs. Jackson by the elbow,

asked her if she'd seen what color the Wimmers were paint-
ing their house, adding that there really ought to be a law. I
let my breath go and gave Maddy an appreciative chuck on
the shoulder.

"What was that for?" Maddy said.

She hadn't yet put it together that she'd just called Mrs.
Jackson's Darlene a slut. She'd simply said what popped into
her head, the bare truth as she saw it. There was never any
acid in her words.

Up and down the street the car engines gunned. We saw
Darlene in sea-foam green climb into an Olds Cutlass, her
skirt twisting around her legs, her high-heeled feet flying up.
Across the street, Stevie held the door for Lynnette. In a tux
he looked like a grown and handsome man, one who could
eat with manners, dance with grace, make love with the
sound of his voice.

"Promenade," Maddy said.

"Promenade?" Tires squealed and horns honked. Buicks
and Fords took off down the street.

"That's where the idea for prom comes from. My grand-
ma told me about it. She said girls used to dress up on
Sunday afternoons and promenade down the sidewalk while
the boys watched, took their pick."

Her voice was dreamy as if she imagined standing in her
front yard, posing for the Polaroid with someone like Stevie
at her side. "Smile," her father would say. "Hold still." The
thought made my stomach fist. I scooped up the car keys

and stood. "You mean whore dogs on parade," I said. "Come on. Let's go."

Maddy looked up at me. Her lips curved into a smile. Plucking her sandals from the porch she said, "Where to?"

I held out my arm, and she took it. Down the steps we paraded, past the shocking-pink blossoms and into a twilight fragrant and lush. I put a deep hip-swivel in my walk. Maddy laughed, then tried it too. We stopped and struck elaborate poses—hips out-thrust, lips puckered, chins high and haughty—as if someone might take our picture, hold us there, just like that, always.

In Creekbaum's Tavern, where Stevie and Winston claimed to have bought magnum bottles of Riunite when they were just thirteen, we picked up a six-pack of Little Kings, then headed for the fairgrounds, me at the wheel. At a red light in the center of town, Bud Sawyer and his cousin Leonard pulled up beside us. Bud drove a Chevy pickup. Zeppelin blasted through their open windows.

"Where you girls off to?" Leonard called.

The pickup was blue with enormous tires and a shotgun hanging in its rear-window rack. Story went that Bud, older than Maddy and me by ten years, had been to jail for hitting a man on the head with the butt of that gun. I didn't know if it was true, but Stevie and Winston always spoke of him in admiring tones: "Bud went wild Saturday night out to Baker's" and "Yeah, he womped on this dude from Black

River" and "You got to watch it with a badass like Bud."

I kept my eyes on the light. To Maddy I said, "Don't answer."

Leonard called, "Aww, come on. Don't be stuck up."

Maddy couldn't bear for anyone to be angry with her or think her stuck up. She leaned over and shouted to Leonard, "We're just headed to the fairgrounds is all."

The light turned, and the Chevy spun out onto Main, then shot away. "Why'd you go and say that?" I asked.

Maddy shrugged. "It seemed rude not to say anything."

"You could have lied," I pointed out, knowing that lying never occurred to her.

"Beer?" Maddy asked, fishing two bottles from the sack and handing one over to me, like a peace offering. Ahead and behind the road was empty. All the way down Route 18 and through the arched fairgrounds gate, we didn't pass a single car, and no Chevy pickup appeared in my rearview mirror. Half the town was at the prom, the rest at Creekbaum's or Timber Lanes, or settled in front of their TVs, waiting for *Dallas*. Maddy fiddled with the radio dial. She hummed to one song, then another. I wondered, stomach tight, how she would spend her summer without me— singing to the radio in somebody else's car, laughing in the deep shade of Darlene's front porch. For the summer I'd taken a waitressing job on Cape Cod in Massachusetts. My mother had arranged it through a friend still prosperous enough to live in Shaker Heights and know about places like

Hyannis. Around Maddy and the others I always bragged and said maybe I'd be serving fried clams to the Kennedys, you never could tell. But inside, in secret, I imagined it this way: the future rolling in fast like the ocean I'd never seen with its mysterious, leg-gripping undertow my mother had warned me about. "Don't go near the water after a storm," she'd said. "Never go deeper than your knees."

"I wish you were going with me," I said to Maddy. I thought if I said it often enough, she just might. We could room together in the boardinghouse where all the waitresses would stay. We could spend our afternoons at the beach and pretend it was nothing new to us. When the other girls, strong coastal-born swimmers all, asked why we didn't venture past our knees and what were we, chickens?, I'd say it was because we didn't want salt in our hair.

"But I am going with you," Maddy replied. She wasn't thinking beyond this night. At the fairgrounds she followed me down the midway to the draft-horse barn. In a wide, open window we sat, drank our Little Kings, and watched the sun slide into a field beyond the fence. The field was just mown, and the air smelled thick and sweetly green. The low white buildings were cast in rosy shadows. On a dozen nights like this Maddy and I had come to the fairgrounds to drink and smoke and talk the future. We couldn't wait for that future to come. Now I wished it never would. I wished the sun would sink and stay there.

"I wonder what they're doing now," Maddy said.

At first I thought she meant Bud and his cousin Leonard. Then I saw the daydream look on her face. She'd had that same look the day before when we passed by the gym, decorated and dark. "South Pacific" was the theme, and the gym was draped with turquoise streamers, multicolored fish, and long-haired mermaids, tiny blue seashells painted over abundant pink breasts.

"Never mind what they're doing now," I replied. "Let's talk about what they'll be doing five years from now."

It was a game we played whenever we needed consoling—the day Maddy learned she hadn't been accepted to any school better than Bowling Green, the time Winston and Robby Junior taped to the seat of my jeans a sign that read *Caution: Wide Load.*

"I'll start." I took a drink, wiped the foam from my mouth. "Stevie Blumenshein will lose half an arm, up to the elbow, in one of the machines at Ridge Tool and Dye."

Maddy considered this for a moment, then said, "Roberta will have four more kids." She shook her head sadly. "None of them normal."

"And one night too many Winston and Robby Junior will get drunk at Creekbaum's," I said. "They'll skid off the curves on Route 58, smash right into a tree."

Maddy looked distressed. "Will they die?"

I shrugged and looked down at the bottle in my hand. "They'll wish they had."

Maddy drew her arms around her ribs, all the warmth

gone out of the night. Side to side she rocked. For a long time, we said nothing. We finished one beer, then another. Silently I tried to imagine a future for us, together, that didn't involve alcohol, babies, and machine-eaten arms: Maddy in a smart navy-blue suit and looking serious over a long line of computers, me at least thirty pounds lighter, living on Cape Cod.

"Are you going to write?" she asked. Her voice sounded hollow, and suddenly, I felt hollowed too. When we were kids, we went everywhere together with arms slung around each other's shoulders. When we stayed over at each other's house, we slept all in one tangle. Maddy always felt so small, just little bird bones, and sometimes I couldn't sleep, I was so scared of rolling over, hearing a little bone go *snap*. This was before we'd learned the dreaded word *lesbian* and started keeping at all times a careful, measured foot between us.

"Course I'll write you," I said. I opened up the last two beers, handed one over to her. Her fingertips slid over mine. They felt warm against the cool, sweaty glass. "I'll tell you about the Kennedys," I went on, "and all about the famous artists and actors and what kind of tips they leave me. And when you come visit, you won't even recognize me 'cause I'll be skinny as a stick, pretty too."

"You're fine the way you are," Maddy said.

"So are you," I replied, though secretly I wasn't so sure, often believed Maddy lacked something basic, necessary, like common sense, like skepticism and reserve. When I was little and my mother would take me uptown, we always passed outside Creekbaum's Tavern a legless old man seated in a lawn chair, an open umbrella hooked to the chair back for shade. "Don't stare; it isn't polite," my mother would hiss, and then she'd draw me quickly across the street as if just looking might take away our legs too. Maddy, though, would have started a conversation with that man. She'd have asked him directly, "So whatever happened to your legs, anyhow?" Better not to think about it. That's what my mother would say. Better to mind your own business; make sure such things don't happen to you. I thought about this now, pitching the empties against the fence, one striking and sounding with a satisfying crack. Maddy gave a little jump as if a gun had gone off.

"What do we do now?" she said. She kicked the heels of her sandals against the wall and looked at me, face hopeful, like I would have an answer. Darkness was settling over the fairgrounds. A light breeze whistled through the buildings, making them seem ghostly. I didn't want to say it: "Go home, I suppose." I didn't want to admit there was no place else for Maddy and me to go, nothing to stop evening from turning into night and night into the next rise-and-shine morning. The sun would pop up and Darlene would wander into my yard sometime around noon. Yawning and stretching, she'd tell me all about the prom. With a honeyed voice she'd say, "So, what did you and Maddy do last night?"

Maddy lifted a finger. "Listen," she whispered.

It was Zeppelin. Faint at first, it grew louder, then louder still. Gravel crunched beneath enormous tires. The pickup rounded the corner. Its headlights glared. Before I could say, "Duck!" or "Hide!", it caught us in its high beams. The beams flicked to low and the volume dropped. I felt the motor vibrate up the wall of the barn, through my jeans, against my skin. Leonard whistled. He said, "You girls ready to party now?" From the window he dangled a fifth of Jack Daniel's.

I pushed myself off the ledge. I tugged at Maddy's arm. She stayed stuck to the wall, stared at me, until I tugged hard enough to bring her down. Forget powder-blue tuxes. We'd be riding high with badasses like Bud and his cousin Leonard. Forget white-coffin corsages. We'd have Jack Daniel's and blasting rock-n-roll. Tomorrow when I'd tell Darlene all about it, every last scandalous detail, my voice would be just as sassy and bold as my mother's azalea bushes. I stood on tiptoe to speak through the passenger window to Leonard and Bud. Yeah, I told them. We're ready. You bet. Then I turned, saw Maddy's eyes stretched wide as moons. "Smile," I hissed. "Look natural."

In the truck I sat squeezed between Leonard and Bud, my legs straddling the stick shift. Maddy sat on Leonard's lap. "'Scuse me," Bud said each time he reached between my legs to shift gears. We bounced over rutted dirt roads: Nickel-Plate, Gore Orphanage, then roads that had no signs, ones

I'd never seen before. Plowed fields stretched on either side, and we'd go miles between houses. Their windows shone black in the headlights. By now it was close to twelve, Maddy's curfew, but she didn't seem to mind. Led Zeppelin still sounded from the speakers, something sad and bluesy. She swayed in Leonard's lap, crooning softly, just a breath out of tune. As we passed along the bottle, Leonard talked nonstop: There'd be a party tomorrow night out to Baker's; Rex McCauley had smashed up his truck for the insurance money; how come we girls weren't at the prom?

"Because, Leonard," Maddy said. Her voice came thick and slow, as if each word took effort to form. "Because, Leonard, we're not sluts."

Leonard put his head back and laughed. "Damn right," he said. When he laughed like that, you could see on one side a gap where a tooth should be. I wondered what that would be like—to lose a tooth, not be able to replace it.

"Maybe you've had enough," I whispered to Maddy the next time the bottle came by.

"Oh, she's all right," Leonard said.

"I'm all right," Maddy said. Her smile was crooked as if drawn with crayon, and her left eye drifted down, the way it did whenever she was tired. I thought of my mother, fuming in the Sunday-morning kitchen about a neighborhood cookout the night before. "I don't care. There's no excuse. Donna Wolstenholm simply should not imbibe like that. Not if she can't control herself." My mother tended towards words like "imbibe" that set her apart from our neighbors who had a good laugh whenever someone managed to get pig-eyed, shit-faced, or drunk as a skunk. "No control," my mother would say, then seal her lips tighter than a lid on a jar. Eyeing Maddy, I felt my mother's irritation crawl up my spine and toward my own tight-pressed lips.

"I'm aaaallll right," Maddy said.

"That you are," Leonard told her. He glanced at me and with a wry smile added, "Very few girls can handle JD like you can." I decided then I liked him. He wasn't a bit like the vague dreams of men waiting for me in Massachusetts, but he offered me Camels and grinned a mile when I told him about Roberta Myers' dress and Darlene with feet flying up. He praised my ability to hold my booze, pick seeds from pot. Maddy's head had listed to the right, and I giggled when he gave her arm a poke.

"Hey, Maddy," I said, poking her arm too. "Wake up, girl."

"Have another drink," Leonard said.

"Or maybe you want a toke instead?"

We laughed hard enough to make the seat creak, but still Maddy didn't come to. Bud said nothing. Even when Leonard spoke right at him—"Hey, Bud, don't you think we oughtta take these girls to the prom?"—he did not say one word. Every now and then he fired up a joint, then elbowed me to take it, pass it down. Though he was sapling thin, I couldn't help but notice his arms. They were hard and muscled. On one arm I believed there was a tattoo—a dragon with a tail snaking down to his wrist—but I'm sure I've made this up. We rode along, the night grown so dark I could see nothing ahead but the yellow-green patch of head-lights, a few odd yards of rutted road. I listened to Leonard. I tried not to look at Bud. My leg was pressed tight against his. My nerves jumped like high-tension lines. I felt the back of my neck all tingly and strange, as if that gun in its rack were trained on me.

"Pretty Maddy," Leonard sang, his voice like a lullaby now. "Oh, sweet Maddy."

Then, at an intersection, Maddy lifted her head. The inter-section was one dirt road dead-ending into another with no signs to mark them. Maddy's hand fumbled about for the door. "Hold on," Leonard said to Bud. "I think this one needs some air." By the time I figured out that I could have said, "Wait, I'll help," Leonard had slammed the door. Bud cut the motor and the lights. There was no more Zeppelin, just night sounds and Maddy retching somewhere down in a ditch. My leg, still pressed to Bud's, had gone numb. I considered mov-ing it, scooting myself over to the passenger door. I pictured myself leaving the truck, holding Maddy's head, stroking her back as she hunched over on hands and knees. I pictured Bud's arms, the snaky tattoo that wasn't even there. In those days I saw danger in the wrong places—in loud claps of thunder, dark spaces beneath beds, in silent men who own shotguns and are rumored to have spent time in jail. I believed too, back then, that ugliness wears an obvious face, a face that was not my own, and that Maddy and I could pen *friends 4-ever* in each other's autograph book and those words would last, a simple truth.

"Do you work?" I finally asked. I tried to make my voice steady, but the words wavered, rose high like birds. He shook his head.

"Laid off?" I asked, then wished I hadn't, though he only nodded and stared, as before, straight ahead.

"Lot of people are," I offered, and he nodded again.

A while later I heard Leonard, somewhere down in a ditch, say, "Hush now, hold still." Then Maddy, voice so slow, "Leonard, what? We go home?" Bud handed me the bottle of Jack Daniel's, and I brought it to my lips. I don't want to say this, but it's true. I held still. I listened hard for Maddy's voice to come again, for the shuffle of sandals on dirt. Nothing. Just crickets and a breeze that rattled the high grass like old bones. I thought then about that man with no legs outside Creekbaum's Tavern. I thought too about flat-eyed babies and Mrs. Jackson's skidmarked face—all those things you weren't supposed to notice, weren't supposed to mention, it wasn't polite, it might rub off. Bud nudged me, and I handed the bottle back to him. He lit a cigarette, offered me one, and we sat there like that, listening, smoking, not saying a word.

Some years later, after my parents' divorce, I went back to Ohio. It was late in May and the last of the spring azalea blossoms were falling away. From the front porch my mother swept the petals with brisk, stabbing strokes, as if they were an affront, something to be angry with. I stayed for a week to help her pack up; she was moving back to Shaker Heights. I saw Stevie, Darlene, and all the rest except for Winston and Robby Junior, who had both died in separate wrecks—Robby Junior parking his car one night, in an error of judgment, on the railroad tracks. I asked about Maddy, who wrote letters I never answered while I was on Cape Cod. Some people said she had married, moved to California. Others said no, it was Indiana, or maybe Idaho. They said, "You look good, Jane" and "You're so thin." They looked at me as if I were proof: money can make you pretty and kind; even this town can have its tales of sturdy, if unremarkable, success. Everywhere I went I watched for a blue Chevy pickup with a shotgun hanging in its rack. Then someone said Leonard and his cousin Bud had gone to Texas; they were looking for work.

When Leonard returned to the truck with Maddy that night, I'd pulled her into my lap and held her there, her head lolling against my chest. Dead drunk, her weight still felt like nothing, and I tucked her blouse into her jeans, rubbed a dirt spot from her cheek, then patted her arm. To Bud I said, "We should be getting back, don't you think?" She won't even remember, I told myself. She couldn't have felt a thing. "Smoke?" Leonard asked me. "Yes," I answered. "Thanks." In my mind I was trying to redo the night, make it bloom a nice quiet pink. Maddy got sick. Leonard took her out, then brought her back. That was all, no harm done, or none that I could see.

Welcome
to the Neighborhood

It came to Allen in a dream, a distant hum that grew as it approached his open window. His current nightmare, a pastiche of the usual anxieties—missed deadlines, sudden hair loss, his wife demonstrating expert skill in magic and announcing her intention to make him disappear—shifted abruptly. Now he found himself in a foreign land amidst dusty camels, striped tents, and colorfully shrouded vendors. He chided himself for being so predictable, even in his dreams.

The hum passed under his window, faded with his dream's raggedy edges. Then came a sudden blast, jolting him from bed, his heart rat-a-tatting until his feet hit the floorboards (smooth, cool wood, not hot, grainy sand), and Allen came to his senses. He was standing by the bed in the only room he and Susan had managed that day to unpack. He was naked before the street-level window. This could prove embarrassing, but he wasn't likely to lose his life. In fact, Allen had never—not even as a teenager under the

influence of grain alcohol or a pretty, unapproachable girl—
placed himself in a situation which might give him a story
to tell, a story that begins, "Well, the closest I've come to
death . . ." There was no firefight, no magician wife. He
turned around to make sure. There was Susan in their bed,
leaning down and patting the floor for her robe. She was
wearing the earmuffs she'd suspected might come in handy,
given the students all around them.

"Welcome to the neighborhood," she shouted, as if she'd
awoken to a wash of bright sunlight and the flutter of but-
terflies.

It was Susan's idea, that first night, to treat it as an adven-
ture. While Allen tried to settle his heart (it danced franti-
cally to the erratic thrash and pound he could not recognize
as music), she disappeared down the hall, then returned
with two plastic cups and a bottle of New York champagne.
After a minute or two, someone turned the music down.
Allen could still feel the bass vibrate through the bedsprings,
but it wasn't disagreeable and the vibrations were starting to
organize themselves into something he could understand as
a rhythm. He heard an occasional whoop. It was three A.M.,
and the students next door were continuing their party on
the porch. Susan spilled some champagne into his cup.

"Just like college, isn't it?" she said. "Except I know your
name."

"Allen," Allen said, though he didn't know why. Maybe he
was half-asleep. Maybe he just wanted to be sure. Once, right

before they were married, they'd run into friends of Susan's ex-husband at the farmers' market.

"This is—" Susan had said, gesturing toward him. "This is—"

Allen didn't find it odd that Susan had forgotten his name. That sort of thing happened to Allen all the time, his own father resorting to "Hey" and "You there." But at that moment, in the middle of the farmers' market, Allen had stood there dumbly. At that moment, Allen forgot his name too.

"Nice to meet you, Allen," Susan said now, tapping her cup to his.

It was pleasant—this festive response to forces beyond their control. Susan swayed to the music. She snapped her fingers, shimmied her shoulders, and said she loved how so-and-so sang such-and-such. Allen decided, as if one could decide such things, that this was the last time he'd dream she'd made him disappear, the last time he'd care if she forgot his name. Their names were together on the mortgage papers, on the marriage license.

Susan pulled off her earmuffs and told Allen a few stories from her college days. She told of one time when a man she'd met in a bar had spent the night, then woke up in the morning and cried, "Shit. My wife is going to kill me." This was before Susan had settled into a set of steadying beliefs involving vegetarianism, weekly recycling, and living in Vermont. Allen made soft tisking sounds. He marveled that any man could wake up beside Susan and not wonder at his luck. The first time Allen ventured to ask Susan out, he was so unprepared for her assent that he'd hung his head and said, "That's okay" and "You don't have to explain."

"I can't believe there's so much of your life I missed," he said now, though he suspected that, back in college, Susan would have noticed him no more than she noticed the dull green paint on the classroom walls. He added, before he could stop himself, "Don't you feel it too? All those years we wasted?"

"Allen, don't," she said. At moments like this, she shivered off his touch the way a horse shivers off flies.

"Look." Her voice was gentle, even, not unkind. "I love you. I wouldn't have married you if I didn't. But I loved my life before you too."

This was one of the thousand nameable things Allen adored about his wife, though it was also the one thing that tugged like a toddler at his heart: she was so perfectly, unflappably balanced. Yet he wanted her to agree that when it came to love, all things should not be measured and fair. He didn't like picturing her choosing between her old life and new as she might choose between cantaloupe and muskmelon at the co-op. When he'd first learned she was a social worker at the homeless shelter downtown, he'd thought she must have an endless capacity for empathy. As it turned out, Susan excelled at her job because she greeted her clients—a necessary, boundary-establishing word—with a vague smile and serene detachment. She made phone calls. She set up appointments. She said, "Good luck!" She said this a dozen times a day.

"It's important," she explained, "that I not expect anything. It's better that way. If by some miracle things work out, I can be surprised."

It wasn't a philosophy Allen could disagree with. From Susan he'd expected nothing at all, and when, by some miracle, she fell in love—"Silly man, I mean with you"—he'd been—oh, yes—surprised. And now, bottle drained and plastic cups rolling on the floor among the boxes, Susan was reaching for him. This always surprised Allen too.

"The window," Allen suddenly remembered. It had no shade.

"What about it," Susan said. "Let 'em look."

Afterwards, she sighed, said she'd die for a cigarette, and promptly fell asleep. Allen listened to the drone from next door and considered again the supreme importance of having no expectations. It was nearing 5:30 when he realized he no longer listened to drunken voices but to early morning birds. He slept, dreamlessly, and when he awoke close to noon, Susan was gone.

That afternoon Allen sat at his computer and wrote just enough to assuage his fears of missed deadlines. When people asked, he said he was a freelance writer. He liked the unlikely image this must conjure up—a man twenty pounds thinner with plenty of hair, dressed in cool khaki, tossing off words for the timid and the frail. In truth, Allen wrote catalogue copy for small colleges and prep schools. He wrote in comfortable clichés that came to him like good friends: *an urban oasis* for a beleaguered Catholic college surrounded by crack houses; *nestled in the peaceful foothills of the majestic Alleghenies* for a school that had received national press when, to escape a hazing rite, a freshman football recruit tossed himself from a high balcony.

When Allen had first taken on such work, he'd tried honesty. About the beleaguered Catholic college, he would have written, *Our students witness firsthand the environmental and human toxicity of the postindustrial landscape that other students in lesser schools only read about in Sociology.* His editor in Normal, Illinois, had returned such copy with a red-penned note, *Is this supposed to be a joke?* On the phone, she said, "Do you know about romance novels? How the hero might be named Lance or Rod and how the soft evening breeze might be infused with the lingering scent of wisteria or magnolia blossoms, but how at bottom, all the stories are the same?"

Allen had nodded, though of course his editor couldn't see him.

"Right," she said. "Well, it's the same for school catalogues. Don't try to be different. We've done the market research, and different isn't good."

Allen was at work on copy for a remote Alaskan boarding

school that promised to rehabilitate the most drug-addicted teen by placing miles of frozen tundra between her and her next score. Naturally, Allen wasn't supposed to put it this way. There was the text, the surface and interchangeable details of mountains and lakes, a dash of culture and an unworrisome pinch of diversity. Then there was the subtext with its whispered promises of loving protection, stern discipline, or whatever it was parents were willing to pay $30,000 a year to get. Allen wrote, *Against the majesty of Mount McKinley, known to the contented natives of this pristine land as Denali, a secluded oasis far from the confusing influences* . . . Then he went outside.

Buying the house had been Allen's idea. He'd felt sorry for it just as he felt sorry for stray cats with scabby wounds. He'd felt sorry for the house but emboldened by it too. A therapist once told him he should stand naked in front of a mirror every morning and say, with feeling, "You have possibilities." Instead, he looked at the house and said, "This has possibilities." Because the house very clearly had problems too, it was the only one in Allen and Susan's slender price range to have come on the market.

"Jesus Christ, Allen," Susan had said, shaken from her usual calm the first time he drove her there.

But Allen hadn't seen the mysteriously missing front steps or heard the troubling buzz from the lights inside. He'd seen instead a column inch of text that began, *A lover's hideaway snugly situated on the northern border of Burlington's historic*

Hill community. The text went on to describe the convenient first-floor washer/dryer hookup, the need for a pinch of TLC and possibly (about this the realtor had been vague) a rebuilt foundation. It didn't matter that Allen recognized all the weary clichés. "Just because our readers can spot clichés," his editor liked to say, "doesn't mean they can't be seduced by them."

Today, as Allen strolled outside, he pictured his house on the cover of a magazine named, say, *Believe-It-or-Not Miracle Home Restorations.* The cover photo featured a rolling green lawn even though Allen's house sat right at the sidewalk's edge, wedged between two neglected Victorians, each carved up into six or eight student apartments. In the narrow strip between the house and gravel drive, the previous owner (who'd sold the house so he could go live on a small island in the middle of Lake Champlain) had planted a strip of hardy perennials. During breaks from his computer and home repairs, Allen could pull a few weeds, spread a little compost, and pick flowers to delight Susan each night. He reached down into the green fronds and pulled up a crushed can of Bud.

"Oh, hey, I'll take that."

Allen turned to face a young man on the other side of the driveway. The young man—just a boy, really—had longish blond hair with tangled curls. He wore cutoff jeans, no shirt, and across his flat belly spread an intricate tattoo. All of the college students these days sported one, and Allen's editor frequently complained about the difficulty of coming up with candid campus shots that didn't require retouching to remove various piercings or fill in bared midriffs. The young man clutched a bulging garbage bag. When he stretched out his hand for the beer can, Allen noticed that his arms were downy and lightly muscled—the kind of muscle developed not by intent but by the simple fact of youth. Allen had never enjoyed such youth. He'd had to start combing his thinning hair sideways before he was out of high school. He went around with his shirt untucked, an unsuccessful disguise for his growing paunch. Allen in bed, Susan liked to say, lying on his back, his great belly bare, reminded her of how happy sea lions like to loll about in the sun. Allen remembered the night before—the festive if flat-tasting champagne, the sweet lovemaking—and he felt grateful to this boy.

"Quite a party last night," he said.

The boy smiled, and Allen appreciated that he had the decency to blush.

"Yeah, sorry about that," the boy said. "Summer session just ended, finals; you know how it is."

"Sure, sure," Allen said easily. "No problem." He liked that the boy had said, "You know how it is" as if Allen had not spent his own college years holed up in a dormitory, reading French surrealist poetry and debating Trotsky's theory of permanent revolution with another equally outcast boy.

"I was once a student myself," Allen said. "If you can

believe it," he added, his voice sounding more uncertain than jovial.

The boy looked at him and blinked. "So, okay, thanks for understanding. Oh, and would you tell Susan we're sorry about the noise?"

"Susan?" Allen said.

The boy was already halfway down the drive, bumping the garbage bag over gravel as if its cans and broken bits of bottles were too heavy to lift. He paused and turned.

"Yeah. Pretty lady with long hair? She's like your girl-friend or daughter or something?"

"Wife," Allen said. "Yes. Susan."

"Yeah, so, she's really cool, you know?"

Allen nodded. Yes, he knew.

It wasn't until the boy had disappeared around the corner that Allen thought to add, shouting after him, "And I'm Allen!"

Early the next morning—very early the next morning—Allen sat in the dark and listened to the voices from the porch next door. Beside him Susan slept or appeared to. The corner of her mouth twitched just slightly when Allen gently lifted the earmuff and whispered, "Susan? Susan, are you sleeping?" He watched her and considered, as he'd been forced to do more and more often, that there were corners of her life she would never invite him to visit. Sometimes she brought him stories from these remote places. The stories always featured *we*—how *we* were camping in Nova Scotia or the time when *we* decided to fly to Lisbon—but the *we* never meant Allen and Susan. It meant Michael and Susan, Burt and Susan, and, in the days before Susan had settled herself down, Susan and some guy whose name she'd forgotten or never learned in the first place because that was the summer she was following the Grateful Dead. Here, *we* meant Susan and Michael. Michael was Susan's ex-husband. Just the week before, a friend casually remarked that she'd spotted Susan lunching with him.

"Ancient history," Susan had said, when Allen brought it up. "Anyway, everyone has the right to go a little crazy once in their lives."

Susan's ex-husband had gone a little crazy when she'd left him. He'd phoned the police, claimed she'd assaulted him, pressed charges against her. Of course the charges had quickly unraveled, Michael blurting out at the arraignment, "This is the only way she'll even see me!" and then demanding that the judge order Susan to remain married to him. Sometimes Allen worried that Susan had married him so soon after Michael because for just that brief period Allen's *un*remarkableness had struck Susan as irresistible. Watching her in the dark, he tried to recall if he'd once gone a little crazy. Crazy is what his father—out of work after thirty years at US Steel and reading in the papers that computers were the next big thing—had called Allen when he'd majored in English at Cleveland State. (Later when Allen landed a tech writing job with a medical software firm in Vermont, his father had slapped him across the shoulders, conceding that "Maybe whose-it here is more on the ball than we thought.") Maybe the craziest thing Allen had ever done was stay in Vermont after the software company folded since Vermont was notable both for its verdant hills and for its lack of jobs. But Allen had just met a woman named Susan who, wonders of wonders, said she couldn't stop thinking about him. Allen had picked up stray copyediting jobs and wondered how long he could make it without health insurance. He wondered how long before Susan would find it perfectly possible to think for long periods of time without thinking of him.

Next door Allen heard the rising voice of a girl, slightly drunk and agitated. "How could you? Don't talk to me!" He shut out the voice and thought about the one serious girlfriend he'd had before Susan. When she left him to marry a truck-stop owner in Lincoln, Nebraska, what he'd felt wasn't sadness or loss but the return of a loneliness so familiar, it had comforted him.

"In front of me too!" It was the girl, louder now, her voice wobbling like an unsteady bird. "It was like you were fucking her right in front of me!"

There was a second voice now, murmuring and low. Its rhythm was slow, soothing, like a porch swing sway.

"Don't touch me!" the girl shouted. "I said don't touch me! *Don't!*"

Allen jumped up, pulled on some pants, and then, re-
garding his belly pale as the moon in the street-lamp light,
grabbed a shirt.

"What's going on?" Susan said. "Where are you going?"

"Fight next door, going to see what it's all about," Allen
replied. He sounded so manly, he almost had to sit down. He
added, hopefully, "Want to come with me?"

"It's just kids," Susan said. She yawned and readjusted her
earmuffs. "Listen. They're already making up."

"I'm sorry," the girl was saying. The birds had left her
voice and now she sounded simply drunk. "I'm sorry, I'm
sorry, I'm sorry."

Allen went ahead outdoors. He was awake and dressed,
and, after all, wasn't this his house? He almost forgot about
the missing front step, then made the leap at the last minute
onto the gravel drive, the stones biting his bare feet. The
word *superhero* inexplicably flashed through his mind. On
the porch next door he saw the blond boy pressed against a
girl at the porch railing. The girl had short, unevenly cut hair,
as if she'd done it herself with blunt scissors. Allen could see
the boy's hands busy beneath her too-tight T-shirt. Allen
didn't mean to, but he stayed there staring until the boy said,
"Hello neighbor. Is there something we can help you with?"

Allen took a step back as if by doing so, he might be swallowed by the night. He made an effort to say, "Thought I
heard something going on. Wanted to see if everything's
okay out here."

The girl twisted around toward Allen. She had piercings on her nostrils and eyebrow that in the porch light looked raw. Allen tried to keep his eyes on her face because just a few inches down, the boy's hands had not stopped moving beneath her shirt.

"So tell him, Devan," the boy said. "Everything all right with you tonight?"

"Beautiful," Devan replied. "Bee—yew—tee—full." She spread her arms wide and arched back over the porch rail. Perhaps it was a good thing, Allen thought, that the boy's hands were where they were since he was preventing her from back-somersaulting off the porch.

The boy pulled Devan upright and regarded Allen, his face bland. Allen decided that he did not like this boy, did not like him at all, just as he did not like Susan's ex-husband, any of the James Bonds, men too handsome, too smug, men without any obvious expectations or anxious hopes because, naturally, they were born to receive all that a man might desire. Devan was giggling, slipping out from the boy's embrace. She whispered something in his ear, then turned on her heel and headed for the door, calling, "Don't keep me waiting."

The boy watched her go, shook his head, and then turned back to Allen.

"There you go," the boy said. "Must have been a dream."

Over the next month, Allen made progress on the house. A carpenter replaced the missing steps. Allen worked through his phobia of hardware stores. While Susan worked at the shelter, he hung curtains he'd found at a garage sale. He might have said this was the first time he actually felt the way men, from all indications, are supposed to feel—capable, decisive, in charge. He might have said this except he was increasingly unnerved by the students next door and, it appeared, Susan was slowly moving out.

It began when she announced she'd signed up for some extra evening shifts. They could use the money, she pointed out, for the mortgage and the repairs. Then one morning he'd caught her at the door gripping a small suitcase, a pillow wedged beneath her arm. Two bright spots appeared on her cheeks and she actually stammered. Sick and amazed, Allen stared at her. Susan had always worn her intentions as she wore her clothes, loose and comfortable, made from natural fibers and vegetable dyes. Now here she was, he was certain, trying to lie.

"I just thought it would be better if I slept there," she said. "For now. We need the extra staff, and—" She paused and they both heard it, a stereo announcing the start to the students' day. "I need to get some sleep."

She kissed his cheek. "I'm sure it'll be better when fall comes. When it's time for them to get back to studying."

But with September, more students arrived, each with a stereo that could shake a stadium. Allen put up the storm windows, and when Susan stopped in to pick up sweaters, he told her the closed windows had helped. Someone next door switched on a stereo. The windows rattled. Susan shook her head.

"I don't know how you stand it," she said. "You really ought to go talk to them." As if all that was needed was for Allen to call a neighborhood meeting.

One night a fight broke out. It spilled into the street and then up against Allen's house. Allen pulled the bed covers over his head and trembled. He no longer had nightmares because he no longer slept, not at night. Even during the day, the students managed to slip into his work: *Whatever spark of esteem our female students have when they arrive is quickly smothered as they learn to allow themselves to be fondled in public. By the time they receive their diplomas, our students are stripped of all remnants of civilization, certified unfit for any sort of occupation.* One time he forgot to delete such sentences from a brochure's final copy, and his editor, who passed the copy on to the school with scarcely a glance, phoned him with a sharp warning. Did Allen realize, she wanted to know, that the company employing him was looking into whether English-educated typists in Mumbai could do this job? Minutes later, a friend called, casually mentioning she'd spotted Susan downtown with her ex. (A few days later the friend claimed to have been mistaken. It was only a woman who'd looked like Susan with a man who'd looked like her ex.) When friends and family telephoned and asked for Susan, Allen had to explain that she had chosen to live, just for now, in the homeless shelter.

When Allen tried, again, to bring up a no-stereos-after-eleven policy, the blond boy said, "Have you considered talking to someone? Like a professional? I did once, and it made me much more sensitive to the needs of others. Didn't it, Dev?"

Though it was chilly and gray, Devan wore a tank top and shorts. She stood, with her long spindly legs, like a stork, one foot tucked up on her opposite thigh. Her skin looked blue. Allen had figured out by now that Devan lived in the house but wasn't really or always the boy's girlfriend. Sometimes he heard them together on the porch, and sometimes he heard the boy out there with someone else. The boy was very popular. A party might die down at midnight, but an hour or two later a dozen kids shouted his name from the street until he appeared like Caesar and announced—what the hell—let the games start again. It wasn't possible that he studied, though Allen wondered if that made any difference to his GPA. Perhaps his teachers gave him A's simply because the boy expected no less. The boy looked at Devan, a look so intimate Allen felt his own cheeks pink. Oh yes, Devan agreed. He was always sensitive, *very, very* sensitive, to all of her needs. The boy looked back at Allen. "So," he said, his eyebrows arched, "how's Susan?"

"Listen," the boy said another time when Allen approached the porch. Devan, or maybe it was another girl, was sulking somewhere in the shadows. The boy's voice was stern as if he were the adult lecturing a teenaged Allen. "This is my home, and I do not appreciate how you continually invade my privacy."

That night Allen called the police. For the first time, he slept blissfully except for one mildly disturbing dream in which he was being chased by angry rabbits. The next day, he felt giddy. He could not wait to tell Susan how he'd brushed his teeth, turned out the lights, and tucked himself happily into their bed while next door two officers had handed out a dozen—maybe more—noise citations.

"Sometimes," he would tell her, his voice firm as a flexed muscle, "you have to use force."

The possibility of such a cozy conversation with Susan wasn't another of Allen's dreams. She had agreed to come over. To talk, she said. Allen ignored her tone. Spaghetti sauce bubbled on the stove. Perry Como crooned from the stereo. Allen crooned too. Backed by Perry and a full orchestra, he heard his own voice as honeyed, persuasive. This whole episode, he decided, would be a funny little story he and Susan would tell, maybe to their kids, the story of how *we* had to get tough with the students next door.

When the knock came, Allen jumped, spattering sauce across his apron. The door was unlocked, and anyway, Susan had a key. It was—still—her house too. He polkaed down the front hallway. He didn't stop singing "Hot diggity dog ziggity . . ." until he swung open the door to find a policeman on his porch. The policeman eyed Allen.

"That your stereo?" the policeman asked. "We've had a complaint."

"Why did you bring the police into it in the first place?" Susan asked him. They were in the kitchen. The noise citation—$75, first offense—lay on the counter. Allen scraped burned sauce from the pan. Susan perched at the edge of her chair as if preparing to rise. "Why didn't you just go over and ask them to turn it down?"

"They're mean to me," Allen replied. He was whining, he realized. He was anything but honeyed and smooth. He kept going. "That boy, he actually told me that I am a very angry man. Can you believe it?"

He stood there, in his apron, appealing to Susan, hoping he looked endearing but suspecting he did not. She was looking at the window beyond him. Allen's garage-sale curtains were white and crisp with a pretty doily edge. Over the apartment window next door was draped the torn image of Che Guevara. Once he'd asked the boy if he knew who Che Guevara was, getting ready to fill him in, loan him books, make peace over the romantic histories of dead revolutionaries. But the boy, in a bored voice, had quickly rattled off a biography plus a sketch of Che's pop cultural appeal, concluding with his own critique of the Maoist belief in an insurrectionist peasant class. Then the boy added, "And how is Susan these days? Oh, wait—I'm sorry. Could it be that she doesn't live with you any longer?" That's when it came to

Allen that all the just punishments he'd planned for this boy were not going to come to pass. If he wanted, the boy would go to med school and graduate too. If he wanted, he would run for Congress and win. If he looked at himself in the mirror every morning and said anything, it wasn't "You have possibilities." It was "You have certainties." It was "The universe bows down before your will." It was "How can we torture our neighbor today?"

Susan took a while considering this last bit, the boy's assertion that Allen was a very angry man. "I wouldn't use the word angry, per se," she finally said. He felt her studying him with a detached air, as if he were one of her clients. "But you have to admit there's a lot going on with you right now. And you're big. Maybe you're not aware of how you come off."

"I'm just trying to make it so you can come back home."

"Actually—" Susan paused. "Actually, I wanted to talk to you about that."

She went on to explain her former relationship to meat—how she'd always thought she wanted it, believed it was good for her, but then, when she became a vegetarian, realized she didn't miss it, didn't need it at all.

"So you're saying I'm like meat?" Allen suddenly found himself thinking about romance novels, about the interchangeable heroes like Lance and Rod. He thought too about Devan next door. He wondered if she would ever claim the power to tell the blond-haired boy, "You know, I thought I wanted you, but then again, I thought I wanted multiple piercings too." Though it was a strange moment to think this, he really hoped so.

"Let's just say," Susan concluded, "that I haven't missed this."

"The kitchen?" Allen asked. "Me? The house?"

Susan shrugged.

"What if we moved?" Allen tried. "A whole new neighborhood, or no neighbors at all?"

"Allen," Susan said. "Our neighbors aren't the problem." Her voice was gentle, even, and not unkind.

This is how it came to be that Allen found himself some hours later struggling through a living-room window. He could have used the front door, but entering through a window seemed to match his clothing (a dark turtleneck, black knit cap pulled snug over his head) and his intentions. He held a pair of wire-clippers, dagger-style, between his teeth. They were the clippers he'd bought at the hardware store on the chance he'd ever get brave about the buzzing lights in his house.

Earlier, he'd watched from the doorway as Susan left. In the driveway, she paused to wave hello to the blond boy and admire some new streaks in Devan's hair. Then she said something to the boy in a voice too low for Allen to catch. The boy looked over at Allen and Allen slunk back, ashamed. *Be nice,* he imagined Susan telling them. *I know he's a pain but he's awfully sensitive too.* One night, he was sure, this image was going to haunt him in a dream: Susan and the blond boy, their heads tilted companionably together or maybe Susan sighing and telling the boy how she'd die for a cigarette just about now. When the music started up—hammering drums and whining guitars that made his fillings ache—Allen considered for the first time that the reason he did not own a gun wasn't because he was a pacifist. It was because he was not.

He knew, of course, he would be caught. He expected it. The students were in the kitchen, steps away, as if the living room's pounding stereo was too much for their ears too. He was already imagining what would come next: Susan, amazed, at the station, bailing him out, or reading about him in the paper. Perhaps he would be heralded as a hero among property owners in this town.

"I'm a felon now," Allen would tell Susan since he was pretty sure that breaking and entering plus property damage must amount to a felony. "Can you ever forgive me?"

In a heartbeat she would, assuring him everyone had the right to go crazy once in their lives, even Allen.

Allen did not know—not then—that Susan had already left the shelter, moved in with the man with whom she had lunched and who really did look a lot like her ex. In this way Susan would continue her life's pattern of drifting back and forth between men who were unremarkable and men who were not. And who would have guessed that while performing the community service to which he would be sentenced, Allen and a compulsive check-forger would fall hopelessly in love? They would take his share from the sale of the house (or what was left after the compulsive check-forger suffered a slight relapse), buy another on that street, living in one of its six to eight apartments, renting the others out to families whose small children would ride Big Wheels up and down the floors over their heads. But all of this was still to come, beyond anything Allen had ever dreamed. The most he could know at this moment—crouched by the stereo, its plug pulled and wire clipped, his heart drumming to a beat that was no longer there—was that finally he too had a story to tell.

The Good Humor Man

The summer our fathers lost their jobs, we all got interested in business. Or maybe *interested* isn't really the word. We felt its presence like a new family on the block, speculated about but not yet spotted. Monday mornings our fathers left on sales trips, worry beading their brows and making half-moons under their arms. With the katydids our mothers began to buzz. *Takeover. Merger. Buyout.* In another ten years such words would become as common as khaki, but back then they came to us, as we slipped in and out through sliding-glass doors, like strange mysteries. *Don't let the air out,* our mothers used to shout. This summer they were distracted. They expressed no interest in signing us up for Little League or driving us to dance lessons. When they stopped reminding us to stay within calling distance, we wavered, fearful of this indifference we thought we'd longed for. We lurked like shy cockroaches at the edge of kitchens until one of the mothers broomed us away. *Go on. Go find something to do.*

Jennifer, the oldest, about to start eighth grade, claimed that if we asked, our mothers would not give us the time of day. "They're becoming liberated," she explained. "That means we're on our own."

"Mom!" cried Jimmy. He was only seven, a wakeup call Dad always said, though it was years before I understood why. Jimmy hurried into the breakfast nook, where the mothers debated the existence of severance pay with the same intensity my best friend Phyllis and I brought to shivery sleepover readings of the Book of Revelations.

"Mom, can I have the time of day?"

We watched from the den—me, Jennifer, Renee Sweterlitsch, the Svoboda twins, and poor Benny Barnhart, whose mother locked him out every morning with just the garden hose for water because otherwise, she declared, he'd cling to her like a baby kangaroo. Around the breakfast table all the neighborhood mothers gathered except Mrs. Paver, who, my sister explained, was *persona non grata*. Mom punched numbers into an adding machine. The other mothers hunched over and peered as if into a Magic 8-Ball.

"Mom," Jimmy cried. "*Mom!*"

In the worn voice of habit Mom replied, "You're in or you're out, Jimmy. Make up your mind."

"Told you," Jennifer said. "I'm surprised she even knew your name." Then she gave him a hug and said, "Listen. Isn't that the Good Humor man?"

Jennifer was like that, seesawing between torture and

consolation. It elevated her status among us. When we felt bad, she made us feel better, and that's what we remembered—the ice-cream cones and pushes on the swing, not the times she persuaded us to slide into sewers or perform mouth-to-mouth on a stiff and glassy-eyed squirrel.

Jennifer, who had recently been allowed to go unsupervised into the adult section of the town library, also served as the official interpreter of the grown-up world and its twisty ways with words.

"Is Daddy getting fired?" Jimmy asked.

"No, honey, that's just a rumor."

"What's a rumor?" Benny Barnhart wanted to know.

Jennifer seemed to give this some thought.

"A rumor," she said, "is a story that's most likely true."

Until that summer we had been middle-class kids, scolded for elbows on tables and stray prepositions at the ends of our sentences. We believed our mothers sprang from their own mothers' wombs fully grown with an exclusive concern for our well-being. We believed sleep-away camp came tucked into summer's pockets along with moon landings and lightning bugs. When our mothers told us that this summer we were going to discover our own backyards, we thought they must mean roller-coaster rides at Cedar Point, camping in the Hocking Hills.

"No," Mom said, pointing toward the sliding-glass door. Beyond the grass baked brown in the June sun. Briefly she tried to put a happy face on our prospects. "You can make your own ant farm," she said. "You can dig to China." Then she went back to taking notes from the newspaper: *recession, inflation, gross domestic product.*

Recession, Jennifer explained to us, meant no trip to Florida's Gatorland. Inflation was why we were made to feel we'd done something terribly wrong if we got holes in our underpants. Meanwhile something called gross domestic product was deflating like a bad balloon, which was why Dad no longer came through the door on Friday nights with jolly jokes about liberals, bra-burners, and other people we did not know. Instead, he muttered about the bosses at Gen-U-Green. He would start with the TV set, talking back to it when he was maybe halfway through his second old-fashioned. His eyes would narrow, staying that way for the whole weekend. Then, from his recliner he would call to us. "How many vice presidents does it take to screw in a light bulb?" he'd bark, or "What do you get when you cross a vice president with a snake?"

He'd always told such jokes to the other dads and even to Gen-U-Green's vice presidents themselves every year at Lawn and Family Day. He'd slap them on the back, ask when they were going to get a real job, then ask if they'd heard the one about the women's libber who wanted to get laid. The vice presidents stood in a line at such events, holding paper plates or cold drink cans in their left hands so their right would be available for shaking. They looked like paper dolls cut from the same sheet. "That's a good one, Wayne," one would say. "You really got us there," another might add.

But lately Dad's tone had changed. His questions felt like tests we continually failed even when we got the punch lines exactly right.

"What do you call a salesman gone bad?" he asked me.

"A vice president?" I'd meant to sound certain, resolute. We had learned this one right along with "Now I Lay Me . . ."

"How old are you?" he asked me another time, after eyeing me over the top of his newspaper.

"Eleven? Almost twelve?" That summer I seemed to have lost the ability to speak to my father in simple declarative sentences.

He scowled. "When I was your age I held down a full-time job. But I don't suppose that's allowed anymore."

I dropped my head, humbled, repentant. I was just out of the sixth grade and had recently faced the fact that I was neither beautiful nor brilliant nor artistic and strange. I was not unique in any way, so I decided to embrace privation as my one shot at an identity. I read *The Grapes of Wrath,* tried sucking in my cheeks and looking gaunt until Mom pointed out that some might think I'd picked up a case of worms playing at my friend Phyllis's. When the Good Humor man came ringing down the street, I turned my back. I pretended not to care.

"Don't be such a puritan, Jill," Mom said.

She looked me over and shook her head. "I suppose you

want to be an actress," she said. "But someone needs to tell you plain, you're just not very good at it."

Pressing dimes into my palm, she added, "Go on. We're not in the poorhouse yet."

We trotted down the driveway, our dimes jingling, Jimmy straggling behind, calling on us to wait up. Then, suddenly, Jennifer stopped. She plunked down on the curb. Just like that, Jimmy and I plunked down too. We stared sullenly at the Good Humor man, his truck with its oversized pictures of nut-speckled drumsticks. On either side of us and across the street Renee Sweterlitsch, the Svoboda twins, and Benny Barnhart did the same. I can't imagine what the Good Humor man must have thought—half a dozen scowling kids, rattling dimes in their fists like goaded snakes. Only Belinda Paver stood at the truck's open door.

"Awful hot out," she said to no one in particular. "I don't see how anyone could pass up the Good Humor man on a day like this."

Belinda was so small and slight, you'd think you could cradle her in your palm like a Pez dispenser. But when she spoke, she used the throaty, teasing, grown-up voice I associated with cheerleaders, movie stars, and girls who'd attended the Barbizon School of Beauty. Her father had been transferred from the Oklahoma office two years before, and when she first moved in, I'd stood round-the-clock watch on her house—that's how much I'd longed to meet this fairy child who appeared just fleetingly, wearing a white tennis dress and perfectly white tennis shoes. For three days, from breakfast to supper, I stayed planted in the front yard, hopeful, anxious, agonized each time the Svoboda twins stopped to say, "She played kick-the-can with us last night" and "She thinks you're a weirdo."

When finally I did make her acquaintance—stepping into the path of her banana-seat Schwinn so that her first words to me were "What, are you a retard or something?"—I had instantly and foolishly offered to give up my best friend Phyllis to become hers instead. Phyllis lived out in the country, and her father did not work for Gen-U-Green. She and her family had a strange set of religious beliefs, associated with being Nazarene. Once Phyllis had seemed exotic, but when I lined her up beside Belinda, I saw that she was hayfield dull, her name embarrassingly old-fashioned.

From the Good Humor man Belinda had selected an orange Creamsicle. As she teased off the wrapper, I felt my mouth go dry.

"No ice cream today," Jennifer told Jimmy.

"I know," Jimmy said, adding, so Belinda could hear, "We don't want to get fleas."

This did not matter in the least to Belinda, who knew she had the power, if she chose to exercise it, to lure any one of us—even Jennifer—into her house for lunch and a look (no touching) at her valuable collection of china-faced dolls. An hour later Mrs. Paver drove Belinda away, off to play most likely with the other vice presidents' kids who lived at Vista

View Estates, where Arnold Palmer was rumored to be interested in a lot and where houses were so big they needed
names. Once I'd gone to a birthday party there. This was
before we kids had clearly and finally sorted into appropriate groups: those belonging to plant workers, to salesmen,
and to management, with the country kids and a few other
oddities sniffing about like strays. At the birthday party
there had been a real pony, a clown, and I think I'd offered
to trade Phyllis in then too. I cringe to consider it, how even
as a child I must have appeared as pathetically needy, grab-
by, a born sycophant. I used to think it was charitable of me,
bestowing my friendship on poor Phyllis. Now I see it was
the other way around.

Gen-U-Green was the only company in Greenville, a
manufacturer of fertilizer, grass seed, and herbicides.
Welcome to Greenville—Where the Grass Is Greener declared
signs at all four entrances to town. The signs spoke the
truth. In Greenville people practiced lawn care like Phyllis's
family practiced religion. Crabgrass and dandelions were
rooted out like sin. The spread of thatch was more feared
than vice. In Greenville Dad was considered a character,
Gen-U-Green's company clown, but I felt sure that when he
called on country clubs from Maryland to Florida, he dis-
played the appropriate reverence—not for the game of golf
but for the grass it was played on. He'd taught me the dif-

ference between fescue and Kentucky blue, how to guard against fusarium blight. Summer mornings the sprinklers rose with the birds, awakened us to their song of *flick, flick, flick.*

Friday nights we met our fathers' cars at the curb. It wasn't that we'd particularly missed them. They'd been Gen-U-Green salesmen since before we were born, and a man home during the week would have been as freakish to us as pot roast on a Monday night. They used to bring us souvenirs—red plastic change purses that puckered up like lips, clear domes making it snow on Hilton Head. Now they brought wrapped bars of Holiday Inn soap, thin towels stamped Best Western. Still we waited, slapped mosquitoes, and speculated about the week's sales. On these numbers, we sensed, everything depended. When Dad's station wagon finally turned in, Jennifer reached his window first.

"Did you meet your quota?"

He was the last father to return since his territory took him from Congressional to Augusta and sometimes all the way to Coral Gables. For a moment he stared blankly at Jennifer, as if she were just more miles of asphalt before him. Then he winked.

"Does a dead man meet his maker?"

He was his old friendly self—the company clown who was also salesman of the year for six years in a row because he could sell fertilizer to places already so green, it hurt your eyes just to look at them. He unfolded himself from the car, and I took one hand while Jimmy grabbed the other. Jennifer bumped his suitcase behind us. Across the street the Pavers' automatic garage doors yawned open. Dad stopped. I felt his body straighten out like a golf club.

"I cut the grass," I told him, tugging at his wrist.

"We showed Jimmy how to do the trimming right this time," Jennifer added, even though she'd just lazed about with a library book she said we were too young for and hadn't helped a bit.

Mr. Paver was moving down his driveway. We could hear his shiny, smooth-soled office shoes on blacktop making a crisp tap-tap-tap. Then came a twang as he gave the for-sale sign a couple of pokes. The Pavers' house had been for sale ever since his promotion—he'd bought a lot out at Vista View—but the only lookers were nosy neighbors since Gen-U-Green wasn't hiring. The Pavers' new house was rumored to be Mediterranean, and it was thought they'd already chosen a name: *La Maison Enchantée* perhaps or *Chateau des Belles Fleurs.*

"Maison a la Fink," Dad would mutter. "Chateau du Knuckle-Tete."

The night was clear and cool, and the air, scrubbed clean by an afternoon thundershower, seemed to magnify every sound—Mr. Paver scuffling his feet, plucking at a weed, clearing his throat. Dad's jaw set and his eyes narrowed without the benefit of two old-fashioneds and the nightly news. I started to tell him about our efforts to aerate the backyard. He raised a hand to hush me.

"What," he said in a voice big enough to carry across a fairway, "do you call an intelligent vice president?"

For a moment there was silence. Then, unexpectedly, behind us, came the sound of Mr. Paver chuckling. "That's a good one, Wayne," we heard him say. "You really got me there." Dad set his mouth into a grimace that would deepen as soon as we got inside and Mom told him the dentist had recommended braces for me. Later that evening Dad called me over to his recliner.

"Well?" he said.

When I just looked at him, he added, "The punch line?"

"An oxymoron?" I tried.

"You're not smiling," he said. "Don't you think it's funny?"

"Yes? No? I don't know?"

He turned back to the TV set.

"Damn right," he muttered, though about which of my answers I can't say.

"I don't want braces," I told Mom. "In some cultures buck teeth are highly desired."

Mom looked up from the adding machine and sighed. She reached into her purse and pulled out three one-dollar bills. "I know you're sneaking your allowance back into my purse," she said. "Now take it. Spend it. We're not in the poorhouse yet."

There really was a poorhouse outside our town. The county home it was called, and when we drove by, Dad would point at its sloping front porch, the shuffling residents who wore what appeared to be bathrobes. "That's where this family is going to put me," he would say.

It used to be a joke. We would laugh, then turn back to the highway that unrolled itself just for us. We would be on our way to a rented cabin in Michigan or Sunday dinner at a restaurant with shrimp cocktail and finger bowls. For those people in the poorhouse, I would feel a moment's abstract sympathy, just as I did at Halloween when I flirted with the idea of collecting for UNICEF. Lately, though, it seemed Dad was making a sincere observation: "We're out of paper towels," "It's supposed to rain," "The poorhouse is where this family'll put me."

Once there, I decided, I would drum up enthusiasm among the inmates for wearing clothes, exchanging slippers for shoes. Under my direction we would invent something useful or start a successful pie factory. Poverty, I realized, only worked as an identity if you could tow yourself out, turn it into an inspiring story to tell. "Now we can get our house back," Mom would sob. Dad would clasp my shoulder, unable to utter a word until I looked up at him, winked, and said, "A feminist, an environmentalist, and a nudist are in a sinking boat . . ." "That's my sister," Jennifer would boast instead of saying, "Eww. Cooties. Keep away." I was the product of too many after-school specials and serial paperbacks featuring clever girl sleuths. I was always trying and failing to start clubs, solve mysteries, save the day.

"We should bring Dad and Mr. Paver back together," I told Jennifer.

"Don't you understand anything?" she replied. "Mr. Paver completely screwed him."

I couldn't deny such a basic fact, and I didn't know how to explain the night I'd spied Dad in our darkened living room where no one ever had any reason to be. He'd parted the drapes just a breath to gaze out at something beyond his reflection. Upstairs, I went to my window, peered out, and there was Mr. Paver. He stood in the center of his drive, shifting his weight from one foot to the other. He was doing nothing purposeful so far as I could tell. He wasn't fixing a lawnmower or counting stars. He was just standing in his driveway, looking at our front door.

It's not just that Mr. Paver had been my father's best friend. He was his only friend since the wit that made Dad the hit of the annual sales convention didn't lend itself to intimate conversations and shared confidences. From Dad, Mr. Paver had drawn out more than the next joke. Side by side on the couch in the den, TV tuned in to the Buckeyes-Wolverines game, they would sing *We don't give a damn about the whole state of Michigan,* then gaze at their beer

cans and speak in hushed, awed voices about men they had
admired, women they had known. When Mom caught me
spying, she scolded me so furiously, I developed a sense I
never could shake that there's something shameful about
two men sharing more than sports and lawn care between
them.

Dad taught trainees like Mr. Paver to chat knowledgeably
with greenskeepers, scoff at the liberal scaremongers with
their exaggerated reports of soil and stream contamination,
sing salesmen songs between one call and the next. He
always wore comic combinations—purple poly golf pants, a
flamingo pink shirt—as if to prove that a man like him
could not be caged, not even by good fashion sense. I used
to believe he scorned offers of promotion, preferring the
purity of life on the road. Now I realize I have no evidence
that offers ever came his way.

"This old hand has been a real father to me," Mr. Paver
had told the vice presidents at Lawn and Family Day, the last,
as it turned out, all our families would attend. This was in
early June, the start of that summer, and Dad's golf shirt had
sported a little picture you'd think was the usual alligator
until you took a closer look and then either tsked or chuckled or looked perplexed, depending on your gender and your
age. Mr. Paver looked as if he'd stepped out from the pages
of a JC Penney's catalogue. Dad slapped him on the back,
said, "Come on, son. Lemme buy you another beer," a joke
because everything at Lawn and Family Day was free.

The next Saturday when Mr. Paver stopped by, his hands thrust deep in his pockets and his smile shaky, Dad had taken the news as a joke, a freshening up of the old *What do you call a salesman gone bad?* All day we watched him bob between indifference and doubt.

"So Brian's ambitious," he tried. "Nothing wrong with that."

He frowned. "But what was that he called me? *Old hand?*"

That weekend the fathers, minus Mr. Paver, had huddled in backyards, eventually concluding that such a promotion couldn't have happened to a nicer guy and that was the damn shame of it. If Mr. Paver had to become a vice president, Dad reasoned, at least he was one who'd stepped on a golf course for reasons other than to play golf. Then came Mr. Paver's first memo. Dad handed it to Mom with a hand that trembled. Mr. Paver, Jennifer explained to us later, had tried to put it into metaphor: for a healthy, green tomorrow, Gen-U-Green might require some careful weeding, a bit of trimming. This was a poor choice of wording on Mr. Paver's part since it implied that our dads could be compared to crabgrass. Jennifer said each of us should solemnly swear to strike Belinda Paver and her family from our hearts. After making us promise not to tell, she let us look at her latest library book, *The Communist Manifesto,* while she explained that our families and the Pavers were now class enemies.

"What if Belinda invites me to play?" I asked. I imagined myself confronted with such a tantalizing dilemma. On one side there would be the tug of loyalty. On the other, the (stronger) pull of desire.

Jennifer rolled her eyes. Everyone knew Belinda had never invited me to play.

It was on this night I spied Dad in the living room, lifting the drape, peering out, wearing that expression I would not be able to explain until I was much older and had seen plenty of Hollywood movies about lost love. For a moment I had thought maybe I should go to him, lay a hand on his arm, speak some quiet words. But I wasn't old enough or of the right sex to say the only thing I'd ever heard anyone walk up to him and say: "Hey, did you hear the one about . . . ?"

For the rest of that summer, our mothers clustered in kitchens. They talked now about getting jobs themselves, starting small. Tupperware? Home macramé? Maid service? A shudder passed around the table since that would mean working for wives at Vista View. Mom punched numbers into the adding machine. They got more ambitious: medical transcriptionist, insurance adjustor.

"What does it say about retirement benefits?" Mrs. Barnhart wanted to know.

"We really need a dental plan," said Mom.

Of course when our fathers came home all this stopped. Each mother stayed in her own kitchen, betraying no interest in the classifieds. Over fences dads swapped tips on bringing backyards back from the August drought. It was as if nothing had changed except that one Monday morning, near the summer's end, Dad trimmed his sideburns, put on subdued, coordinating colors, and tossed his purple poly golf pants into the bag marked for Goodwill. When he left with the rest of the dads for a special meeting at Gen-U-Green, I thought he looked smart, like he'd just stepped from the pages of a Penney's catalogue. It was some years before I would understand his change for what it was—desperation, like Mr. Svoboda using the twins' college fund for a membership at Vista View Country Club or me jettisoning all the pride I'd been born with the day I crept across the street and left in Belinda Paver's mailbox a note: *Will you be my friend? Yes. No. (Circle one). P.S. Please say yes!*

When our fathers returned home an hour later, we were sitting cross-legged in our front yard while Jennifer read to us from *Silent Spring*. The day was hot and hazy, and we might have sat there for hours, too lulled by the cadence of her voice, the tickle of Gen-U-Green grass against our thighs to even notice when Jennifer closed the book and said, voice soft, "I think it's our dads she's talking about." As our fathers pulled into driveways one by one, each leaving his separate car and walking silently, slowly into his separate house, we watched as if this too were a dream. One by one, Benny Barnhart, Renee Sweterlitsch, and the Svoboda twins drifted away. It's as if we never saw each other again. By winter, all of us were gone to Indiana, Wisconsin, and Alabama, later to Michigan, Pennsylvania; who could keep track? For a year or two a box of note cards, unopened, sat on my desk, a farewell gift from my best friend Phyllis, who had hand-stamped each one in vacation Bible school. Then the cards disappeared, lost, I suppose, in our next move.

Dad was the last to return. He unfolded himself from the car and looked at us, blinking. Then he winked. It might have been another Friday night, just another homecoming. Except it was Monday, it was morning, and when Dad spoke—"What do you call a salesman gone bad?"—he whispered.

Later, in college, I would learn our fathers were not remarkable but part of a statistical set, the last to believe that fidelity defined the relationship not between a husband and wife but between a man and his company. I would learn that our fathers had been replaced by a far superior being, New Economy Man, more flexible than a Slinky, able to bounce from job to job like a happy rubber ball. From Gen-U-Green my father had bounced to a fertilizer plant in Minnesota and then on to Indiana, to a factory that produced packing peanuts. He tried once to explain to me the superiority of packing peanuts over bubble wrap but gave up mid-sentence. A well-packed box had nothing on a well-kept lawn. It was Mom—who became a girl Friday, going to school nights in one state and then another to eventually earn an associate degree in computer programming—who wound up with a happier tale to tell. She even had the luck to cash in her company stocks just before the market, and the company, went bust. And I mustn't leave out Mr. Paver, who has recently risen to the top of the *New York Times* best-seller list with *Better Business Ethics: Transforming Corporate America into a Venue for Virtue.*

"Pig," says Jennifer, who openly admits to shoplifting the book from an airport paperback rack. Jennifer belongs to an anarchist environmental group. She makes headlines for stopping bulldozers with her body and tossing pies at politicians. She is the grown-up version of the clever girl sleuth, and sometimes I think I've spotted her on the news, though it's hard to tell with the black bandana. Mom says we are not to tell Dad, who stopped watching the news when Walter Cronkite retired. Both have stopped asking if I'm seeing anyone. It is always Belinda Paver all over again: *Do you love me? Yes. No. (Circle one.)*

"Are you saying we know him?" Jimmy asks. He examines Mr. Paver's picture on the book cover—youthful face, genial eyes, hair showing a few well-placed and reassuring touches of gray. Jimmy hardly remembers Greenville. He travels a lot these days with his new job. When people ask him where he's from, he says, "What state are we in now?"

"Let me see that," Dad says from his recliner. There's some shuffling, some hesitation, and then Jennifer hands the book over. Dad looks at Mr. Paver as he sometimes looks at us, his expression blank. Jennifer and I sigh out our relief. Brian Paver no longer rings a bell. A minute later he's dozed off, lightly wheezing. We've come home—Florida now, not Ohio, Minnesota, or Indiana—to help Mom pack up. It's too hard for her, looking after Dad, so she's decided they will move together to assisted care.

"Hey," Jimmy says as we turn toward the kitchen. "Did you hear the one about—"

Jennifer groans. I roll my eyes. Jimmy is such a joker. He's got a million of them.

"Oh God," says Jennifer. "Here we go again."

About the Author

Nancy Welch was born in Florida and grew up in Ohio, Michigan, and Minnesota. She was a secretary and police reporter before finding her way to college and to writing fiction. Her stories have appeared in venues such as *Prairie Schooner, Threepenny Review,* and *Greensboro Review.* She teaches at the University of Vermont and lives in Burlington.